"DOG GONE CHRISTMAS"

Other Books
By Terry I. Miles

"I'll Love You Till You Die"
"Death Has No Appeal"
"Laughing All The Way", A Christmas Tale
"Say A Little Prayer for Me"

"DOG GONE CHRISTMAS"

A COZY LITTLE MURDER MYSTERY

*SET IN AND AROUND BAY ST. LOUIS
FEATURING
MAGGIE MAY (THE DOG)
OF MAGGIE MAY'S ART & GIFT SHOP A
Novel*

Terry I. Miles

iUniverse, Inc.
New York Lincoln Shanghai

"DOG Gone Christmas"
A COZY LITTLE MURDER MYSTERY

Copyright © 2006 by Terry I. Miles

iUniverse books may be ordered through booksellers or by contacting:

iUniverse
2021 Pine Lake Road, Suite 100
Lincoln, NE 68512
www.iuniverse.com
1-800-Authors (1-800-288-4677)

This is a work of fiction. All of the characters, names, incidents, organizations and dialogue in this novel are either the products of the author's imagination or are used fictitiously.

ISBN-13: 978-0-595-41098-9 (pbk)
ISBN-13: 978-0-595-85457-8 (ebk)
ISBN-10: 0-595-41098-7 (pbk)
ISBN-10: 0-595-85457-5 (ebk)

Printed in the United States of America

In Memory
And Dedication

On June 11, 2006, our friend Kay Miller was murdered in Biloxi, Mississippi. She was a lover of the Arts and participated by attending the theatre and concerts plus an avid reader of books. Kay's regular attendance of church and Sunday school was an inspiration to us all. Her ready smile and friendship will be sorely missed.

Therefore, this Christmas novel is dedicated to her memory.

We miss you, Kay.

For Your Information

On June 11th, 2005, Bay St. Louis held Second Saturday from 4 p.m. to 8 p.m., like every Second Saturday since the beginning of the year. I had been invited to have my book signing for my second book, *"Death Has No Appeal"* at Maggie May's Art and Gift Shop, on Main Street.

What an exciting time! I naturally wanted to make a good impression, so I arrived early and set up my assigned corner with my books, advertisement posters and gift cups.

John Brennan and Dave Moynan III, the proprietors of Maggie May's Art and Gift Shop, gave me the printed story of how the store received the name of Maggie May. A lady of eighty-nine years of age, did not like her friends suggestion of turning her dog over to the SPCA, since she would soon be residing in a nursing home, so she put her dog out on the street with a note.

When John and Dave were out walking with their own dog, Beardog, he and Maggie May made eye contact. After discovering the note, they took her home and named her Maggie May.

After my book signing that afternoon and evening, John asked me if I would like to return at Christmas time for my Christmas book signing of my third book, *"Laughing All The Way", A Christmas Tale* and then he added, "Terry, could you write a story about Maggie May, for next Christmas, to which I replied, "Sure!"

The next afternoon, June 12th, I began writing my cozy little murder mystery about Maggie May and her abduction! Later on in the months of June, July, and up to August 20th, I wrote my little tale about Maggie May, Bay St. Louis, and my two protagonists, Bea Winslow, Private Investigator and her Aunt Jewels.

The last time I went to Maggie May's Art and Gift Shop, was on August 20th, to pick up the three early drafts of the manuscript. (I gave John and Dave and their saleslady Barbara, one each to read). They thoroughly loved the story and couldn't wait until Christmas of 2006 and the premier book-signing at the shop on October 14th, the second Saturday.

Of course, August 29 [th]**, at 7: 30 a.m., Hurricane Katrina unleashed her fury along the entire Mississippi Gulf Coast.** The beautiful houses, quaint shops, and businesses located along Beach Boulevard and Main Street in Bay St. Louis were demolished, ravaged and gutted. Only broken asphalt, concrete, sand and mud replaced the once gaily lit stores.

Everything was gone! Eighty percent of the damage was done to Bay St. Louis and Waveland, Mississippi.

The pictures located within this book are those of my June 11th book signing and of the devastation of property after the worst storm in history. I was also granted permission by Mr. Stan Tiner, Vice President and Executive Editor of The Sun Herald, to include four pictures consisting of Main Street, before and after, Dock of the Bay and the Bay Town Bed and Breakfast, Bay St. Louis, Mississippi taken by John Fizhugh, photographer and a written caption by Kat Bergeron about how Bay St. Louis is recovering and the observation of their first 'Second Saturday', October 8th, 2005, after the storm. Included are my pictures that I snapped that afternoon of October 8th, 2005. Also are pictures of 'Second Saturday', May 13th, 2006.

Therefore, I decided to go ahead and publish the Christmas story about Maggie May and Bay St. Louis. I certainly hope you all enjoy it!

Maggie May's Story

On All-Saints Day 2002, Maggie May bounced into our lives. Beardog, our 13 year old Chow/Shepard mix, was out for an earlier than usual morning walk to accommodate our plans to visit the cemeteries and leave mums for all our loved ones passed.

As we neared the local coffee shop Bear stood up extra straight and started wagging his tail furiously. He and Maggie May had made eye contact. While they said then* 'hellos' I asked around to find out who the short black dog belonged to. The response was the same each time I asked: *0h, that's the dog with a note on its collar. Been hanging around all morning."

Hours later, after taking both dogs home (Beardog was hopelessly in love) and visiting the cemeteries we finally read the note. The note, pinned to her collar, began, "I'm 89 years old and dying…" and went on to talk about the dog's favorite food, date of birth, and the owner's hope that someone would find her and love her since she herself could no longer keep her.

So we kept her. And we named her Maggie May.

Now, with the sale of each Maggie May t-shirt, we make a contribution to the Friends of the Waveland Animal Shelter so that every little black dog left on the street might have a chance at finding a home.

Acknowledgements

The writing of a novel involves many, many people. You might agree it is like **growing a flower.** First you have the ***germination*** of an idea. For this book, that idea was formed in June, 2005 by John Brennan and Dave Moynan III. They encouraged me to write about their dog, Maggie May.

The story began to take ***root,*** growing a little at a time, day by day. After two or three months, I assembled the first draft and took it to John, Dave and their part time associate, Barbara, for a read through. They loved it! Since we were going to present it for Christmas 2006,1 thought we could work on it a little at a time, plus I was finishing and polishing my novel for the spring of 2006.

Hurricane Katrina roared ashore on August 29th, 2005, leaving the entire Mississippi Gulf Coast in shambles! Bay St. Louis and Waveland, Mississippi were almost wiped off the map! Storm surge and wind ravaged Beach Boulevard and Main Street, depositing sand, asphalt and cement where music, art and laughter had reigned supreme!

I decided that very day, I would continue on with my novel about Maggie May being kidnapped, along with my protagonist, Mrs. Julia McKenna. Her niece Bea Winslow, a Private Investigator, Sheriff Jim Travis of Lafouchfeye County and a host of fictional Bay St. Louis policemen and women come to a climatic rescue!

Of course, the ***first bud*** of my 'flower' goes to Richard and Dee Cichon, those dauntless proofreaders and scanners. The ***individual petals*** belong to Evelyn Hinton for her patience in accompanying me over to Bay St. Louis for picture taking, Jon Davidson on his mortuary expertise and Vicki Niolet for her encouragement. I would be remiss if I forgot artist Sylvia and Bill Stanton. They were very helpful with history and background.

Also, providing the **<u>stem</u>** and **<u>leaves</u>** are four important staff members from The Sun Herald Newspaper. I was granted permission by Mr. Stan Tiner, Vice President and Executive Editor, and his administrative assistant, Janine Harges, to include four pictures of Bay St. Louis, Mississippi. These were taken by John Fitzhugh, photographer, of Main Street, before and after, the Bay Town Bed and Breakfast and the Dock of the Bay. A written caption by Kat Bergeron about the history of the Bay Town Bed and Breakfast plus how Bay St. Louis is recovering and the observation of their first 'Second Saturday', October 8th, 2005 is included.

Definitely **_the full glorious bloom_** would go to the publisher iUniverse and their staff.

So during this Christmas season, take time to count your blessings, have a cup of hot cider or eggnog, enjoy this cozy little murder mystery and **_stop and smell the roses!_**

Synopsis
"*DOG Gone Christmas*"

Seven years ago Horace Fletcher, Director of Shady Rest Funeral Home, was found dead at his desk by the housekeeper, Maudelle Perkins. Cyrus Dedeaux, one of three morticians hired by Mr. and Mrs. Fletcher, was declared guilty. However, new DNA evidence, presented by his lawyer, had proven Mr. Dedeaux innocent and he has been set free!

Three days after Cyrus returned, there has been an alleged attempted murder on Rose Fletcher, Horace's widow, and a body has washed up on the beach.

Before attending the gala benefit honoring environmentalist, Dr. Horatio Banks, in Bay St. Louis, Mississippi, Mrs. Julia McKenna and her boyfriend, Captain Eric VonBoatner, are supposed to pick up a 1927 Model T. Ford, which she won two months earlier in a drawing.

During an impromptu shopping spree, Aunt Jewels and a dog named Maggie May are kidnapped and dog napped respectively. Upon inspection of the floorboards inside of the antique car, her niece, Private Investigator Bea Winslow, discovers small specks of dried blood.

Mystery, mayhem and merriment, follow these two sleuths as they weave their humor, crime solving tactics and hilarious antics, through a host of unsavory characters, the funeral parlor, saving the environment, Christmas festivities in the Bay......and finding Aunt Jewels and......Maggie May.

Prologue
"DOG Gone Christmas"

December 1998 Shady Rest Funeral Home
On the Edge of Lafouchfeye County

"Where have you been," Maudelle hissed. "I've heard something!"

Cyrus stopped in his tracks and listened. "I don't hear nothin' and besides…I'm here now baby," he cooed, then passionately kissed her.

She sharply pushed him backward. "This is the last time you convince me to meet you here, at the Funeral Home…"

Cyrus pulled her close once more and nuzzled her earlobe while squeezing her waist. "We have it made here. No one's going to bother our 'little love nest'."

Cyrus Dedeaux was an excellent mortician, but a lousy husband. His wife Gigi, was working the late shift at The Tiny Diner and had been for three months now. Business at the Shady Rest Funeral Home had been slow and all three morticians, Cyrus, Tommy and Bubba, had their hours cut back. Since Tommy Lockhart was in college, it gave him extra time to study and Bubba Cuevas just liked the free time to spend fishing. Maudelle's husband, Charlie was a card dealer in Biloxi, at one of the local Casinos. He had injured his back five months ago and had just recently gone back to work. Oh yes, it did happen on the job, and because Charlie had taken a swing at another man for looking at Maudelle. Still, Maudelle convinced him, that in order to catch up on their bills, she would have to get a job. Cyrus had taken a special shine to Maudelle since her first day as head of housekeeping at The Shady Rest Funeral Home, owned and operated by Horace and Rose Fletcher.

Pearl Rooster, Maudelle's older sister, owned the beauty shop two doors down from the funeral home. She had been the Fletcher's hairdresser for the deceased, for the last ten years. So naturally, Rose Fletcher had confided in her as to their desperate need of a head housekeeper. Pearl instantly thought of Maudelle. It would certainly help out her financial situation, at least for a little while.

Mr. Tom Malone, Superintendent of the Highway commission had promised both Mr. and Mrs. Fletcher and Pearl Rooster to tell them of the decision on where the new highway was going to be built. The Shady Rest Funeral Home and Pearl's Beauty Shop were the last two businesses to buy up.

"This place gives me the creeps, Cyrus. All these dead bodies lying around."

"You got that right, Maudelle. They're not standing up! Anyway, the only two here now are what's left of that couple from the house fire, over by Vancleave road, you know."

"What are you gonna do with them?"

"Gee whiz Maudelle, get your mind back on what we were doing, okay?"

"There it is again!" Maudelle whimpered.

This time Cyrus also heard the noise. "That sounded like it came from the front. Maybe the old man came back to his office. Go look and see."

"Not on your life, Cyrus Dedeaux. Not by myself! You're comin' too!"

"Okay, okay, we'll go together." As they slipped through the dimly lit parlor rooms, the killer had carelessly dropped a plastic Cruisin' the Coast button on Horace Fletcher's office carpet, when heading towards the front door. Now the shadows of Cyrus and Maudelle slowly crept along the long hallway leading to Horace Fletcher's office. His door was wide open. Horace was seated in his large wing back chair, behind his desk, facing the rear window.

Curious, but cautious, Maudelle moved closer. "Mr. Fletcher," she whispered, "I didn't realize you were working late. Mr. Fletcher?"

When he didn't respond, Cyrus walked around Mr. Fletcher's desk and saw the bullet hole in his chest. "He's not talkin', babe, cause he's dead."

"Oh my God!" screamed Maudelle. "Someone's killed Mr. Fletcher!

CHAPTER 1

Seven Years Later December, 2005

"Aunt Jewels, where's this morning's paper?" Bea asked while coming in the kitchen door. "Aunt Jewels, did you hear me?"

"I heard you, I heard you," she shouted back. "Yes, I got the paper and was reading about Cyrus Dedeaux being released from Parchman Prison three days ago." Putting her hand over her mouth, she muttered, "Oh dear Bea, that's when Rose Fletcher contacted Sheriff Travis about discovering poison in her coffee cup at the funeral home!"

"It wasn't poison, Aunt Jewels, only loose tea. That's not why I wanted the paper. Sheriff Travis called me last night and told me some other startling news."

Aunt Jewels immediately lowered the paper, and looked directly into Bea's eyes. "What startling news?"

"Do you remember a fire seven years ago, Aunt Jewels?"

"You're talking about that house over near Vancleave road. Yes, what about it?"

"You recall, they supposedly found the remains of two bodies."

"Go on Bea...."

"Well, Horace Fletcher took care of those remains."

"Well, yes, but he died almost ten years ago..."

"Seven years ago, Aunt Jewels. And another thing, Jim, Sheriff Travis, was called and told of a body washing up on the beach, near Espy Avenue in Long Beach early this morning. Naturally he called his long time friend, Dr. Nathan Tate, the New Orleans coroner."

Aunt Jewels sat there, staring at Bea. "Bea dear, why do you continue to call Jim 'Sheriff Travis'? You have been seeing him for over a year now. I would think you would be on a first name basis!"

"Well I declare!" Bea exclaimed. "I certainly didn't realize I was on some sort of time schedule as to when I should call the Sheriff 'Jim' instead of Sheriff Travis. But since we happen to be on this subject, I recall you sometimes refer to Captain VonBoatner as Captain Eric."

Aunt Jewels sat there thinking. "All right Bea, I suppose you have your reasons. Let's change the subject. You mentioned he called Dr. Tate…well, the coroner of Lafouchfeye County was there also, right? Any identification?"

"Yes, of course Aunt Jewels, Betsy was there and to answer your second question, no, none yet."

"Look dear, I don't want to put a damper on all your and Sheriff Travis' findings, but……"

"Well, Jim, also mentioned Tom Malone was back in town, asking again about The Shady Rest Funeral Home and Pearl's Beauty Shop."

"Look Bea, I have to get ready for Captain VonBoatner, I mean Eric, to pick me up. Remember, we're going to the big Christmas environmental benefit on the back deck of The Dock of the Bay in Bay St. Louis today. Dr. Horatio Banks is the guest speaker!"

"My, my Aunt Jewels, if you hadn't gotten your hair done yesterday, at Pearl's, you would be chomping at the bit to ride with me and talk this over with Jim."

"Well, I do have a social life, you know dear."

"What time will the Captain be arriving?"

Aunt Jewels looked at the kitchen wall clock and then at Bea. Two seconds later, the phone rang. "I'd estimate his arrival in the next……twenty-five minutes! Bea get that phone, will you?"

"Okay, but old girl, you'd better shake a leg! Hello? No, she can't come to the phone at present. May I help you, I'm her niece. What? Oh my word! Yes certainly, I'll let her know. In fact she will be coming that way to hear Dr. Banks speak. Oh yes, she'll be surprised! Bye now. Aunt Jewels?"

"What is it Bea?"

Quickly Bea walked towards the first landing of their staircase. Aunt Jewels peered over the top banister and asked, "Who was on the phone?"

"Some gentleman called Amos Seals the spokesman from *Cruisin' The Coast*. It seems you have won a Model T. Ford."

Aunt Jewels cautiously scampered down the steps toward Bea. "What? The handyman from the bed and breakfast? Good gracious dear, I registered for that several months ago!"

"Well, Aunt Jewels, his explanation was they had made a mistake. Your ticket was stuck to somebody else's and well…he simply apologized. In fact if you like, he said you and Eric may pick it up this afternoon at the Bay Town Bed and Breakfast, across from The Dock of the Bay."

"Did I hear someone drive up?"

Bea turned around on the landing and looked out the bay window. 'It's the Captain. Better hurry up Aunt Jewels!"

CHAPTER 2

Maudelle and Charlie

As she rolled over in the queen size bed, Maudelle thanked God for finally having a day off.

"Maudelle!" Charlie yelled. "Maudelle!"

Slowly she crawled out of bed, threw on her chenille bathrobe and wearily dragged herself to the front porch. "What are you yellin' about Charlie?"

"I was just readin' the paper and thought you might like to know, that 'friend' of yours is out of jail. Got out three days ago."

Maudelle yanked the paper from his hands and slung it towards the porch steps. "Don't you think I already knew it? For heaven's sake Charlie, he worked at the funeral home!"

"Look here woman," sneered Charlie, while pushing his wheelchair to face her, "it ain't my fault my legs failed me!"

Maudelle spun around and faced him. "It ain't nobody's fault. Mine, yours or your Aunt Minnie's! If you need something I'll get it for you, but if you don't, I'm goin' back to bed. We had to decorate for Christmas and clean that place up spic and span like, for those inspectors this past week and I'm tired!"

"Okay then," said Charlie. "Would you mind bringin' me that little cell phone, just in case I need it?"

Maudelle turned and disappeared into the house. Soon she was placing the small phone on his lap. "Here you are. Now please, let me get a few more hours of sleep and then I'll fix us somethin' to eat."

Charlie watched her, as she walked away, and thought back to their happier times. At least they were happy times for him. He was never sure about

Maudelle. Nine years ago he had met Maudelle at The Hole in One Bar, on Cainey Creek Road. She and her sister Pearl were bartending. At first, Charlie made a play for Pearl and she had been receptive, but later when he spied Maudelle, well…let's just say he changed his mind. After several dates, he asked her to marry him. Charlie would have given Maudelle the moon, if she asked him to. After they got married, Maudelle seemed distant and depressed. About three months later, Maudelle told him she was leaving. Charlie went nuts! He told Pearl when he found Maudelle, he was goin' to kill her! Maudelle stayed gone for six months and then one day, Charlie heard the front screen bang and there she was. He was just so happy to see her, that he didn't care that she had been gone. Now she was back.

Of course he was jealous. He always had been. He started gambling all of his paycheck and soon they were in debt. It was the night that Maudelle came to the casino and sat down at his dealer table. This handsome guy started eyeballin' her. Charlie lost it right there, and decked the guy. During the brawl, he hurt his back and was out for five months. Maudelle told him she'd get a job and when Pearl told Mrs. Fletcher, well, Maudelle became the head housekeeper for the funeral home.

Charlie knew that somethin' was goin' on, because Maudelle was makin' excuses for this and that. That night, seven years ago, when she was late comin' home, Charlie went down to the funeral home and Maudelle's Ford was parked at the far end of the parking lot along side a burnt orange pick up truck. He knew whose it was. That Cyrus Dedeaux. Charlie started sneakin' around the back of the building when he discovered a side door unlocked. Quietly he stepped into the pitch-black room. Suddenly, a blow to his back, with a blunt instrument, sent him spiraling to the floor! When he tried to move, he couldn't! Now he heard voices. That was Maudelle! How was he goin' get back to his car? Slowly he dragged himself out the door to the parking lot and then collapsed!

Later that evening, when he awoke, Maudelle and Dr. Wills were standing there, lookin' down at him, lying prone in the bed. Dr. Wills told him his spine had been severed. He would be confined to a wheelchair the rest of his life.

CHAPTER 3

Tom Malone

"Hello? Oh, it's you. Yeah, Merry Christmas. Look, I told you I'd take care of it! I got into town two days ago…you know that. Calm down. No, they know nothing, trust me. Bye."

As Tom Malone closed his cell phone, he sank into the maroon leather chair. He had been the Highway Supervisor for the past seven years and had made quite a name for himself. He was twice nominated and received Supervisor of the Year, and saved Lafouchfeye County four million dollars in construction materials.

Thanks to Aunt Betsy, the present coroner for Lafouchfeye County, who was his deceased father's sister, plus his excellent grades had enabled him to attend Thaddeus Revere Academy, in Revere, New Hampshire on a full scholarship. In his Junior year, after exams, his roommate William Dubois, invited Tom to his home for Thanksgiving dinner. Seated across the elegant table was William's sister, Crissy Dubois. Of course at first he thought she was just an opinionated female from an aristocratic family. To some extent, that was true, however, beneath those golden curls and deep blue eyes, beat a heart of deceit. After four more years of college, he received his Engineering Degree, and they were married.

Once more he opened his briefcase and took out the proposal papers. It was a good offer. An excellent offer. Both the beauty shop and the funeral home would prosper from the sale. Of course he understood Pearl's reluctance and thought of their last conversation in which she revealed her difficult life. The summer that Pearl turned sixteen, her father, Pappy Rooster, hired a drifter, to help him with the inventory at his country store. He called himself Joe. No last name, just Joe. It was an instant attraction between Pearl and Joe. Nine months later, Pearl delivered twins, a girl and a boy. Pappy was furious and threatened to kill Joe. Of course Pappy was unaware that both his girls and Charlie had witnessed his outburst of anger. The next morning, he told Pearl, Joe had left.

Raising two children had not been easy for Pearl. Every once in awhile, Maudelle and Charlie would step in and help, but those times were few and far between. No, Pearl struggled along, helping her dad in the store and attending night classes to obtain her GED. The five of them, Pappy, Maudelle, she and the children, had lived in the store's back quarters. After Pappy Rooster passed and Maudelle married Charlie, Pearl took her share of the insurance money and went to beauty school and then renovated the country store and opened up her own beauty parlor.

Suddenly the ringing of the motel room phone interrupted Tom's concentration.

"Hello? Pearl, it's good to hear from you. Yes…you sure can. See you here at seven this evening. Bye."

He had no sooner hung up the phone when his cell phone chimed. Looking at the number, Tom smiled to himself. "Well, hello there. I was wondering when I was going to hear from you. No babe, not tonight. I have an important meeting. It's been a long time for me too. Miss you? You bet I miss you! Look sweets, if this deal goes through, you and me will be sitting on easy street, sipping those little drinks with the umbrellas in them. Save me some sugar……sugar. I love you too. Bye now."

CHAPTER 4

Aunt Jewel, Bea and Captain VonBoatner

"Well now, don't you look like a dapper Dan," Bea smiled, as Captain Von-Boatner came sashaying through the kitchen door. "I must say, you two make a handsome couple!"

"Hush now, Bea," winked Aunt Jewels, "you'll make Eric blush!"

"Soooo, what all are you two going to do over at The Dock of the Bay?"

Eric squeezed Aunt Jewel's waist. "Now Bea, you know your Aunt. She's adamant about saving the beach and stopping the erosion, so that's why we are attending this lecture by Dr. Horatio Banks."

"You remember him, don't you Bea, dear?"

"Of course I do. How could I forget! I went to school with his son, Horatio Jr. I told Sheriff Travis, I mean 'Jim', about the lecture and he said we would see you there later on."

"Wait a minute," Eric replied. "Are you talking about the man who invented the microchip lever for the upcoming space shuttle launching at Cape Canaveral?'

"The one and only, Eric dear," Aunt Jewels cooed. "Bea and I had lunch with him six months ago."

"Julia," began Eric, "you never cease to amaze me!"

"Well, actually it was Bea he invited, but I went along. She received an award for her investigative service. He really is a nice gentleman. You know he lost his wife last year."

"You don't say. Sorry to hear that," Eric replied.

"Yes, it was sad news."

"Still, I hadn't realized. The man's a genius!"

"Well you two had better be going or you'll miss the first part of the lecture. Jim and I should be leaving shortly. We'll see you there, bye now!"

After the Captain's car had pulled out of the driveway, Bea's fax began buzzing and humming. She shrugged her shoulders while approaching the vibrating machine. It was from Sheriff Travis.

"I'll be there in a second. Tying up some loose ends here at the office. Oh yeah, got a fax from New Orleans Police, Security Police at NASA, Bay and Waveland Police. Extra Security will be placed around the outside lecture area for Dr. Horatio Banks. Oh, by the way, did you know that Horatio Banks, Jr. was one of Cyrus Dedeaux's lawyers? See you soon."

"Now that's very interesting," muttered Bea.

CHAPTER 5

Maudelle

"Come on….come on…," Maudelle mumbled. "Answer your phone, Pearl!"

"Pearl's Beauty Salon…may I help you?"

"Pearl, it's me, Maudelle. Whatcha doin'?"

"I just this minute finished a shampoo and set, why?"

"Would you go with me to the lecture that Dr. Horatio Banks is givin'?"

"Gosh Maudelle, I'd like to, but I'm seein' Tom in an hour."

"Tom Malone? He's in town?"

"Yeah…"

"Don't tell me you're sellin'….1 don't think you should."

"Why not? The kids are gone and I'm ready to retire."

"What about the funeral parlor? You're not doin' the dead peoples hair anymore?"

"Tom offered Rose a good price too. I think she's gonna take it."

"You know of course, you could hold out a little longer. Maybe they would kick in some more bucks!"

"Maudelle, I've lived in this place all my life. I've worked hard. I would think you would be happy for me."

"Pearl, I'm happy for you, but you don't…."

"Maudelle! Who the hell are you talkin' to?" Charlie yelled.

"Is that Charlie screamin' at you?" Pearl asked.

"Yeah…pay him no mind. Well, I better go. Please Pearl, don't sign any papers till I get back from that lecture tonight. Promise me that."

"Why?"

"Just promise me Pearl…"

"Okay….bye."

"Maudelle!" Charlie screamed again.

"What do you want now?"

"Who were you talkin' to?"

"My one and only sister!"

"What's her problem?"

"Oh, nothin'."

"Gotta be somethin'. I haven't seen you this upset in a long time."

"Look Charlie, I'm gonna change and go to that lecture in Bay St. Louis. You want me to call Deputy Paulie to come over? In case you need somethin'?"

"How long you gonna be gone? What lecture?"

"I don't know. Maybe two hours. Dr. Horatio Banks."

"Right! The guy that's gonna save the world. How come you're goin'? Since when did dirt interest you?"

Maudelle turned around and smirked. "Since I've been workin' at the place that shoves them in the ground. Now, do you or do you not want me to call the Deputy?"

"Okay…okay, call him! But I want you back home at a reasonable time."

Maudelle's voice trailed behind her, saying, "Sure Charlie…anything you say Charlie," as she climbed the old worn wooden steps to her bedroom. She also thought about Pearl and the beauty shop……and another set of wooden steps……

CHAPTER 6

Pearl's Children
Timmy Rooster and Mae Beth
(Rooster) Ladner

Tomorrow morning the Greyhound bus would be pulling into Bay St. Louis and Timmy Rooster would be home for the first time in three years. Of course, Pearl, his momma, thought he had been working in El Paso, Texas. That's where all the postcards came from. No, Timmy had been doing time for 'obstructing justice'. At least that's the way they put it in Alabama, His sister, Mae Beth had married an Army boy, from the Kiln, Mississippi, by the name of Chester Ladner and he was stationed at Fort Bliss, Texas. Anyway, he was going to surprise his momma with a visit.

He certainly looked different, that was a fact. When he left, his small frame hardly even filled out the patched up overalls. Now however, breaking those Alabama rocks had produced muscles in his shoulders and arms. The deep brown hair had streaks of blonde through it. Toiling in the sun all day had produced that and bronzed his chest. Yes, Timmy Rooster had left a boy, but now he was a man.

Mae Beth had gotten pregnant right after her sixteenth birthday. Of course it broke Pearl's heart when she told her. The wedding was a small one, just Pearl and Maudelle. Mae Beth always sent a Mother's Day card though and she made sure Pearl got one from Timmy also. Now Mae Beth had two kids herself and Chester was gone to *Iraq*.

She was surprised to hear her momma was selling her beauty shop though. Tom Malone had tried to buy it twice before, but she always refused, so it sort of surprised Mae Beth when she received her momma's short note, sayin' she had made up her mind.

Mae Beth remembered when Tom Malone was in town the last time. Of course that was seven years ago. She was workin' as a waitress at the Tiny Diner with Gigi Dedeaux. When he came in that evening, Gigi remarked, "you know who that is?"

Mae Beth recalled that she giggled, and replied, "oh sure, the great Tom Malone, the savior of Lafouchfeye County. Who doesn't know him?"

"That's not what I'm talkin' about, you silly girl," smiled Gigi.

"Oh yeah?"

"Yeah! Word has it, he has a girlfriend back here."

"You don't say...who?" Mae Beth asked.

"Well now, I'm not sure, but I think it's......"

"Hello Ms. Gigi," replied Tom, "and who might this pretty little girl be?"

"My name is Mae Beth, Pearl Rooster's daughter."

"Pleased to meet you Mae Beth," Tom winked.

Two days later, they were parked on a dead end gravel road, south of Ghost Bayou Park. Mae Beth began teasing him. "Won't your girlfriend be jealous?"

"I don't have any girlfriends, except you and I certainly don't need anymore in my life."

"Don't you forget me Tom."

"I told you, as soon as I can, we'll get married."

"Listen, I'd better get back. Momma will have the dogs after me. When you comin' back honey?"

"As soon as I can, sweetheart. Now straighten yourself up."

The wailing of her second baby brought Mae Beth back to reality. What began to trouble Mae Beth was hearing from some of Chester's kinfolk that the new highway was gonna be built at the edge of LaFouchfeye County and some people were gonna make a bundle of money. "So that's what Tom Malone is up too," she whispered, while rocking the baby. "Well, we'll see about that." Quickly she dialed her momma's telephone number. After ringing five times, the answering machine kicked on. "Please leave your name and number. I'll get back....I promise."

CHAPTER 7

Bea Winslow and Sheriff Jim Travis

"I was wondering when you were going to arrive Jim," Bea smiled, while greeting him at the kitchen door.

"Sorry I'm late Bea, but I got the word back on our body that washed up on the beach."

"Well?"

"Horatio Banks, Jr. Cyrus Dedeaux's lawyer. They're trying to locate Dr. Horatio Banks now."

"Well Jim, that shouldn't be difficult. The man is going to give a speech in late afternoon in Bay St. Louis, remember?"

"Bea, at the present time, Dr. Horatio Banks can't be found."

"What do you mean, he can't be found?"

"Well, Stennis Space Center faxed Bay St. Louis and Waveland Police, that the Doctor had left the Space Center. They were supposed to pick up the cavalcade when it reached Highway 603. It never arrived. Listen, that's not the only thing."

"There's more?"

"Sure is. Remember seven years ago when that house burned on Vancleave road?"

"What about it?"

"Supposedly Horace Fletcher handled the ashes found. You know, the two bodies. Well, I got an anonymous phone call. It was a woman's voice, telling me the man was alive and she was sending me proof. Federal Express delivered a package today consisting of fingerprints identifying the man as Curtis Burras, from Canada. He's a well to do land developer and get this....Tom Malone know him very well."

"Okay Jim, let me get this straight now. The washed up body is Horatio Banks Jr., his father is missing, and you received a package from somebody telling you a dead person is not dead, but alive and Tom Malone knows him. Correct?"

"What? You don't believe me?"

"Oh I believe you, Jim. If Aunt Jewels could hear this, she would go wild!"

"Isn't she with Captain VonBoatner?"

"Yes she is. In fact she told me that 'she had a social life'. *So*...what do you wish to pursue first?"

CHAPTER 8

Bubba Cuevas

Bubba Cuevas had secrets. A lot of them. In fact, he was at The Shady Rest Funeral Home that evening, seven years ago, when Horace Fletcher was killed. He saw Maudelle and Cyrus makin' out in the autopsy room and he heard Maudelle's husband Charlie, drive up. Yes, Bubba knew a lot, but the killer didn't even realize Bubba was around. In fact, the moon was so bright that night; Bubba saw the killer push the 1927 Model T. Ford to the edge of the parking lot, and then crank it up.

Just because Bubba was heavy and had a baby face, people assumed he was a teddy bear. Actually it was just the opposite. Sheriff Travis had jailed him five times for assault and battery. It was Pearl Rooster who consistently bailed him out. Bubba took it real hard when his momma died in that train wreck seven years ago. She was comin' home from visitin' her sister in New Orleans and had the radio goin' full blast. She died instantly. Of course her services was held at The Shady Rest Funeral Home and Rose helped out tremendously. Since Cyrus was in prison, Tommy Lockhart and Rose Fletcher did the embalming. It was a beautiful service. Everybody attended. There were a few people Bubba didn't recognize, especially a young man that stood at the rear of the parlor room. Bubba noticed Horace's killer was courteous to all the towns-people. No, thought Bubba, this is not the time for confrontation. He would let his grief heal and then, later he would spring his surprise.

When he had gotten a haircut at Pearl's Beauty Shop earlier, she had mentioned Tom Malone's offer and asked his advice. "I'd sell," his reply had been.

Of course Pearl had no way of knowing Bubba Cuevas was looking forward to his share of the money. Yes siree Bob, Bubba would definitely buy a large boat and spend the rest of his life fishin'!

CHAPTER 9

Eric and Julia

"You look especially marvelous Julia," smiled Eric.

"Why thank you, kind sir. I try my best! Oh look Eric, there's a parking space in front of the Bay Town Bed & Breakfast. Park there." Aunt Jewels loved the Christmas decorations that adorned the quaint lamp posts. Everywhere she looked, sparkling lights twinkled.

"Now Julia? Don't you think we're early?"

"Of course, we are Eric, but I would like to shop around. You don't really mind, do you? It's so festive! I mean, I like to show off the man in my life."

"Well, since you put it that way, how could I refuse you!"

"Okay then, let's walk down the street. See….over there is The Dock of The Bay and Dr. Horatio Banks is having his lecture on their deck. He is such a tremendous influence, don't you think?"

Eric smiled. "I said he was a genius. What more could I add?"

"Oh look Eric…that's a fanciful little shop. Let's stop in there."

Since there were several shops nearby, Eric stopped and looked around, and then asked, "where, Julia?"

"Silly, over there. Across the street. Maggie May's."

As Eric opened the door, a tiny jangle from the attached bell announced their arrival. Soft lighting and the scent of evergreen welcomed them. The store was tastefully decorated with Christmas artifacts, paintings, perfumed soaps and pottery. An attractive lady around forty, greeted them from behind the well stocked counter. "Good afternoon. If I can be of any assistance, please don't hesitate to let me know."

"Thank you," Aunt Jewels replied. "Isn't she gracious, Eric?"

Eric smiled at both ladies and proceeded to amble over to admire some hand made pottery. Suddenly a squeal from Julia made him turn his head. "What is it?"

"Oh Eric, dear, come here and look at this precious dog. I wonder if it's a girl or a boy."

From out of the next room came a tall, lanky gentleman, grinning from ear to ear. "Oh, I see you have met Maggie May. My name is John."

"This is Maggie May?" Julia questioned.

"It most certainly is. Here, let me get you her history," and quickly moved to the far end of the counter. As he handed it to Julia, he replied, "I'm sure you'll find her story interesting," and then disappeared through a side foyer.

After the two of them glanced over the article, Julia remarked, "Oh Eric, I would like a dog like her. Look, she likes to be petted. You are just a darling...I wish I could take you home with me."

The ting-a-ling of the little bell caused everybody to look towards the door and that included Maggie May. One man was dressed in a three-piece suit, crimson tie and matching handkerchief. The other three were casually dressed in khaki pants and polo shirts. However, Julia's keen eye spotted several revolvers, tucked in hip holsters underneath their lightweight jackets. Eric grabbed Julia's arm and nudged her over to a display of candles and blown glass. The four gentlemen were headed directly toward the counter.

"Yes sir, may I assist you?" Asked the saleslady.

"Do you have a convenience room we may use?"

"You mean a rest room?"

"Yes ma'am."

"Through that door and to your right," she pleasantly spoke.

"Thank you," replied the sharply dressed gentleman.

Meanwhile, Julia was eyeballing all of them, twisting this way and that.

"Julia," whispered Eric, "what are you doing?"

"You have never met Dr. Banks, right?"

"No."

"Eric, that was him....I don't know who those other guys are, but something is wrong."

The snappy dresser pivoted around and bent down to pet Maggie May. "Is this your dog ma'am?" He asked Julia.

"Oh, no sir. She belongs to the proprietor of this shop. Pardon me, aren't you Dr. Banks?"

As he started to speak, one of the other heavy set gentlemen pulled on the older man's arm, jerking him up.

Julia whispered, "Eric, I think," as she gripped the corner of the nearby desk....

"I think....," interrupted Eric, while helping her to stand, "your imagination is running away with you again. Look, it's almost time for Dr. Bank's lecture. We had better be heading across the street."

When Julia's eyes scanned the shop, she looked puzzled. "Eric, where did everybody go? I know that was him..."

"I'm sure the owners and the sales lady have stock to count and put up. Come on now, or we'll be late. The 'gentlemen' probably left by the rear exit."

"Okay......, if you insist."

After Eric escorted Julia out the door, he encouraged her to quicken her steps. Suddenly she stopped and felt her earlobe. "Oh dear! I've lost my earring! Bea will kill me Eric, because I borrowed hers. I bet you it's in Maggie May's bed. "You remember," she said with pleading eyes, "when I bent down to nuzzle her neck. You wait here, I won't be a second!"

Eric looked up at the blue sky, rolled his eyes and heaved a heavy sigh. "Go, if you must."

The sharp jangle of the little bell brought no one through any of the adjoining doors. Quickly, Julia hurried over to Maggie May and began rummaging through her assorted blankets and covers. "It must be here, somewhere," she muttered to herself. What's this, she thought, twirling a small metal circle-like battery.

Suddenly one of the men Julia had noticed earlier came running through the back archway and quickly proceeded to lock the front door.

"What on earth are you doing?" Julia demanded, while she struggled to stand up.

"Grab her, Meathead and...the dog!" Maggie May began barking! "They're comin' with us!"

"Oh no you don't!" yelled Julia, as she reached for and grabbed the dog.

Immediately the man produced a rag and jammed it over Julia's mouth and nose, rendering her helpless as Maggie May slipped to the floor. As Aunt Jewels hung there, lifeless in his grip, he asked, "now what do we do with her, boss?"

"Take her out back and put her in the car! I'll bring the mutt!"

"What about the other two men and that lady?"

"Leave them tied up in the bathroom!"

Due to the activity outside of a group of carolers and strolling minstrels in the street, Eric didn't hear the commotion from inside the shop, nor the click of the front lock. He stood patiently, arms crossed, shifting his weight from one foot to the other, pushed back his sleeve, and looked at his watch. Now, glancing over his shoulder, he thought, what was keeping her? He retraced his steps and tried the door. It was locked! He yelled, "Julia?" Again he pulled on the door! A curious crowd of people began gathering and a policeman was among them.

"Is something wrong sir?" The officer asked.

"My name is Captain VonBoatner, Eric VonBoatner, and my lady friend and I were just in this shop. She thought she lost her earring and reentered the shop to find it. Now the doors are locked and I don't see her!"

CHAPTER 10

Gigi Dedeaux

When Cyrus was convicted of Horace Fletcher's murder, Gigi promised him she would wait. Now, seven years had passed by. What she didn't add at the time, was to remain faithful and keep her wedding vows. Gigi wasn't stupid. She knew Cyrus was seeing somebody, but she didn't know whom. At one o'clock on Saturday afternoon, Gigi went to Pearl's Beauty Salon and had her hair done. On this particular Saturday, which was one week before Cyrus returned, Bubba Cuevas came in all tuckered out from working, and wanted a haircut. He told them about a bad wreck off Highway 13 involving five cars and a dump truck. The ambulance had brought three people into the funeral home. Tommy, Rose and himself were all working on bodies at the same time. Well now, Bubba had a slip of the tongue, so to speak, because he mentioned Maudelle as the lover Cyrus had been seein', before he went to prison. Pearl caught Gigi squirming in her chair a bit, and whispered, "Gigi, be still now."

Well, that just confirmed it. Gigi was going to move up in the world and she knew just who to contact too! So, by the time Horatio Banks Jr. got Cyrus out of prison, Gigi was a different person. Oh, she was still married to Cyrus, but in name only.

When Cyrus arrived home that Sunday before Christmas, Gigi was poised and waiting at the bus station to meet him.

When Cyrus spied her petite figure standing on the cement platform, his jaw dropped. Slowly he mouthed out loud, "Wow! Gigi, you look terrific! Your hair....that outfit...man...I have missed you!"

"I bet you have Cyrus Dedeaux and you know what? You're goin' to miss me some more! Here are the divorce papers, just sign'em, because I'm through with you!"

"Aw! Come on Gigi! Have a heart!"

"Get Maudelle to have a heart!" and off she strutted, shaking her booty, just like a dressed up hen, paradin' around the chicken coop.

CHAPTER 11

Tom Malone's Motel Room in Lafouchfeye County

Wheel of Fortune was just going off the television, when there was a light rap on Tom Malone's motel door.

As he opened it up, he expected to see Pearl Rooster. It wasn't.

"Merry Christmas sugar, may I come in?" she replied politely.

Tom smirked a little. "As much as I would like…you can't, honey. I'm expecting to close a deal. A very important deal. We can make it later."

"Okay then, but don't forget me."

Tom's eyes covered her from head to toe. "Oh, don't worry baby, I won't forget you," and watched her sashay away in her tight fitting lime green knit dress around the corner. He took a quick glance to either side of the parking lot, just to make sure no one was around, and then closed the door. Once more he settled down on the edge of the bed and looked at his watch. Pearl seemed to be running a little late. Then a knock on his door startled him. He jumped up and peered out the bent blinds. It was Pearl.

"Come on in dear and have a seat. I was beginning to wonder…."

"If I had changed my mind?" Pearl smiled. "I'm breakin' a promise to Maudelle. I told her I'd wait."

"Pearl, you're doing the right thing. I wouldn't steer you wrong. Now let me get those papers from my briefcase. Since your establishment is located on the corner, your settlement is somewhat higher than Rose's. Let's see here, okay....you need to sign here, here, and here. By the way, did you bring your papers?"

"Yes, Tom...I have them right here in my purse." Pearl slowly withdrew the sheath of papers, took a deep breath and held them close to her chest. "You know of course, this place has been my entire life. A lot of memories, both good and bad are wrapped up in those four rooms."

"Pearl," replied Tom, "initial here. I came from humble beginnings also. If it hadn't been for my dad's sister, well, I wouldn't have had the opportunity and education. Oh, initial here also."

"And," Pearl added, "you wouldn't have met that sweet wife of yours. How is she Tom?"

"Crissy? Oh, never better. She's quite a lawyer herself, you know."

"Really? What kind of lawyer?"

"She deals in taxes, mostly. Well, let's get to signing these papers!"

Just then there was a loud pounding on Tom's door. As he swung it open, Maudelle shouted, "Is Pearl here?"

Tom stepped to the side and Maudelle stormed into the room. Seeing her sister sitting there with the pen in her hand, disappointment filled Maudelle's voice. "Pearl, you promised to wait."

"I'm sorry Maudelle, but I've already signed the property over to Tom."

Maudelle sank down on Tom's bed and just stared out the window.

"Did you like the lecture Maudelle?" Pearl asked.

"What?" said Maudelle.

"Did you enjoy Dr. Banks' lecture?"

"Oh, he didn't show up, for some reason. I don't know why."

"Well ladies, I hate to leave such good company, but I do have another engagement, so if you don't mind, I'll see you later Pearl when the demolition starts in two days."

As Pearl stood up, she glanced at the muted television. "Look ya'll, that's Bea Winslow, the Private Investigator. What's she saying?"

"Let me turn it up," Tom replied.

"We have a kidnapping which took place about an hour ago. My Aunt Julia McKenna and a dog called Maggie May from Maggie May's Art and Gift Shop in Bay St. Louis, Mississippi. Also at this time, Dr. Horatio Banks has disappeared. He was last seen leaving his office at The Stennis Space Center, coming to lecture at The Dock of the Bay, on the back deck. Sheriff Travis and Deputy's Paulie and Taylor of Lafouchfeye County are questioning the proprietors and saleslady of Maggie May's Art and Gift Shop that were found tied up and gagged in the restroom. Now we'll return to your regular scheduled program."

CHAPTER 12

Christmas Is A Week Away Somewhere Off of Highway 603

"Hey Mousy, that broad is comin' to!"

Aunt Jewels tried to adjust to the darkness by blinking her eyes.

"Well now, I do hope you're feeling better. I am sorry about our friend Meathead, roughing you up like that."

"Just what is it you're after?" Aunt Jewels asked, while rubbing her head.

Mousy smiled and then quickly laughed hysterically. "Dear, dear woman, you really don't think I'll tell you now, do you?"

"Well sir, all I was after was the earring I must have lost while petting Maggie May. They belong to my niece, you know. So I really don't know why you have me half trussed up like a calf at rodeo time!"

"Look ma'am, I really don't want to hurt you, so just be quiet and we'll try to have you home by Christmas."

"That's next week! Now you see here....1 demand to be let go! My niece is Bea Winslow, the Private Investigator and her boyfriend is the Sheriff of LaFouchfeye County, Sheriff Jim Travis! If you don't want all thunder and damnation to rain on you..."

Suddenly Meathead wrapped his arm around Aunt Jewels' neck and put a sleeper hold on her.

"Thanks Meathead, she was beginning to get on my nerves. Now give her dose of chloroform. That will put her out for a couple of hours."

"Did you hear what she said Mousy?"

"Don't tell me you're worried about a little P.I. and a redneck Sheriff?"

"Mousy, I don't want to go back to the slammer at Parchman!"

"Don't you worry, you won't be goin' back! Those high falootin' guys know what they're doin'. How's that dog comin' along?"

"Aw, the mutt is okay and so is the doc."

"Has he decided to talk?"

"Naw…he hasn't said nothin'."

"Does he know about his son?"

"Don't think so…."

"Well……casually mention it to him.…tell him the same thing could happen to him."

"But Mousy, if we knock him off, how we goin' find out where.…?"

"Look Meathead, it's a ploy.…."

"What's a ploy?"

"Never mind…just put the old broad back in the side room, on that mattress."

"Look at her Mousy…she looks like an angel lying there."

CHAPTER 13

Gerald Sheppard,
Also Known As,
Curtis Burras

"Fasten your seatbelt sir," The stewardess pleasantly spoke, "we'll be landing at Gulfport-Biloxi International Airport in fifteen minutes."

"Thank you ma'am," Gerald Sheppard smiled. The smoothness in his speech caused the stewardess to take a second look at him. He was good looking and dressed for success in the dark grey suit. Land investments and real estate had been his scam since his first contract in New Orleans, Louisiana. After graduating from engineering school, he was introduced to Horatio Banks, Jr. at a cocktail party being held by Tom and Crissy Malone. Crissy's cousin, Darlene Dubois was visiting and a foursome was arranged for the following evening. The chemistry between Darlene and Gerald sparked and six months later, they were married in a lavish wedding at his father-in-law's beachfront property. A honeymoon in Europe followed.

Gerald's lucrative work flourished over the years and provided Darlene with expensive houses, jewelry and....many acquaintances. However, Gerald never seemed to complain of her nocturnal visits and stay over's with her 'sick Aunt'. For you see, Gerald had his own agenda.

This particular plan had been in operation for the last seven years. Of course, Horace Fletcher stumbled onto the scheme and had to be eliminated. Actually, the scheme was Darlene's idea. Have a fire and destroy everything, including her and me. She was absolutely correct in her research. Find two vagrants, a man and woman, hopefully our same weight and size. Invite them for supper and lodging and then kill them. Burn them and the entire house. Everything must go. Having already acquired false birth certificates, driver's licenses and bank accounts, Darlene and I would vanish from Vancleave road and establish our residency far, far away. I agreed. It was a damn good idea and I told her so, right before I killed her. We had made sure our 'replacements' were drunk and asleep.

Darlene was so methodical in her placement of our 'bodies' and kitchen rags. She laughed while she made sure our suitcases and documents were secure in the front porch Oleander bushes. Upon her return, I encouraged her to relax, have several shots of bourbon, before I finished the 'deed'.

"We've had a good life, haven't we?" I asked.

She tilted her head back, while she swallowed the shot of bourbon, causing her wavy russet brown hair to shimmer in the lone candle's light. "We certainly have, my dearest."

"Here," I added, "have another shot. You deserve it."

Quickly she tossed it down and then slowly lowered the small glass, until it rested on the wooden table. "Are you purposely trying to get me drunk and......take advantage of me?" she snickered.

"No," I replied, "actually I'm feeling a little guilty and sorry that I have to do this."

"Do what?" she blinked.

"Kill you Darlene."

She tried to stand up, but slumped back down on the chair. "Why?" she asked, while her eyes tried to focus.

"Because," I began, "I figure with everything burnt, including you, they will have to do forensic identification through DNA and bone tissue. Well dear, it will seem more authentic if they find that you really did die in the fire. Therefore, the authorities will assume I'm dead also."

"No! Please Curtis......don't do this!!!"

"Goodbye, Darlene......"

CHAPTER 14

Sheriff Travis, Bea Winslow and Captain Eric VonBoatner Outside of Maggie May's Art and Gift Shop

"All right Eric," Bea replied, "tell me again. Exactly what happened to Aunt Jewels?"

"Like I told you before Bea, Julia, your 'Aunt Jewels', discovered one of her earrings was missing. She was upset because she knew you would be, so she turned around and hurried back to the shop. When she didn't return after 5 or 10 minutes, I was concerned, so I walked back to the front door of the shop. It was locked. I yelled, Julia? No response. I shook the door. That's when this policeman approached me."

"And your name is?" Bea asked.

"Barney Frye, Officer Barney Frye, Bay St. Louis."

"Officer Frye, this is Sheriff Jim Travis, Lafouchfeye County, you know Captain VonBoatner and my name is Bea Winslow. I'm a Private Investigator and Mrs. Julia McKenna's niece."

"I've heard about you Sheriff Travis and you too Ms. Winslow. Nice to meet y'all."

"What happened next?" Bea inquired.

"Well ma'am," Officer Frye replied, "I called for backup and Captain Von-Boatner and I went around to the back entrance. It was wide open. Officer Daniel Sign and Officer Maddie Trace arrived…."

"And who are they assigned to?" Bea questioned.

"Bay St. Louis police, ma'am."

"Continue, please…."

"I told the Captain here, to wait outside and the three of us entered the back of the shop."

"Then what happened?" asked Sheriff Travis.

"Well sir, we found the two owners, John and Dave and their assistant Barbara, bound and gagged in the bath room. Maddie, I mean, Officer Trace, helped them out of their tape and ropes. Officer Sign and I checked out the entire store and found no one. After that I went and told Captain VonBoatner."

"Okay," said Bea. "Only a couple of hours have passed since they kidnapped Aunt Jewel's and the dog. Let's go in and talk to John, Dave and Barbara."

Unfortunately, for the prospective customers, the police wrapped a yellow crime scene tape around the entire building and posted two policemen, one at the front and back of the store. Both the owners and their assistant were sitting huddled together at a little mahogany table, each holding a cup of tea, in various positions. Bea couldn't help but think of a similar pose.

"Hello there," smiled Bea. "How are y'all doing?"

"What on earth is going on, ma'am?"

"And you are?"

"I'm John and this is Dave. Our part time cashier is Barbara Monti."

Bea took out her notebook, flipped it open and began writing down their names. "Well John, that's why the Sheriff, myself and Captain VonBoatner are here. I certainly don't know why anyone would take your dog and my Aunt Jewels. But I can guarantee you sir; we are going to get to the bottom of this dilemma. Now, what can you tell me?"

John looked at the other two and then began speaking. "Ms. Winslow, your Aunt and this gentleman came in and I showed them the little paper we have written up about our dog, Maggie May. Then four gentlemen came in through the front door."

"What did they look like?" Bea inquired.

"The first one was a sharp dresser. Steel colored white hair and tortoise type glasses. The other three were attired in sport type clothes. They asked Barbara to use the rest room…"

"John," interrupted Barbara, "He said convenience room, I assumed he meant rest room."

"Yes my dear. Now to continue…the sharp dresser turned and went back towards our dog, Maggie May. I heard him ask your Aunt if it was hers. She replied no and pointed towards me. I was standing in the back doorway," and he gestured in that direction. "The next thing I knew a gun was in my ribs and I had joined Dave and Barbara in the bathroom, tied up and gagged."

"Did you hear them talking…or anything?"

"Yes ma'am, I did. One was called Mousy and the other's name was Meat-head. They also mentioned a computer chip or battery."

Bea, Sheriff Travis and Captain VonBoatner turned around when they heard the commotion at the shop's front door.

Officer Barney Frye was courteous, but firm. "I'm sorry sir, this is a crime scene, and you cannot cross."

"I'm Barry Luce with the Naval Investigative Service, Stennis Space Center and these are my two associates. Who's in charge here?"

CHAPTER 15

Jeannie Rose

Lots of things had changed, since that misty December night in 1998, seven years ago. Running away from their abusive Aunt and Uncle was Bennie's idea. So Jeannie Rose and her brother Bennie had traveled by bus from the delta to Hattiesburg. Of course what little money they had left was spent on food, so they began walking.

When they approached the Vancleave road turnoff, there she was. Bennie said it was fate that brought them all together that night. Naturally when the pretty lady offered them supper and lodging for the evening, they jumped at the chance. She called herself Darlene and his name was Curtis. I remember asking her why she was walking. Her explanation was simple; their car had broken down.

Our supper consisted of ham and butter beans, cabbage, cornbread, ice tea and bread pudding for dessert. During our dinner Curtis keep filling our wine glasses. There must have been some knock out drops he had added. Bennie drank more than I did, but I was certainly woozy. Of course neither one of us knew then the purpose of our visit.

Two, possibly three hours had passed and Darlene encouraged Bennie to go to bed. I remember vaguely sitting in a comfortable chair in the living room. Darlene was talking about kitchen rags and bodies. Then it was deathly still and quiet.

Suddenly I felt myself being picked up and slung around. It was cold and damp. I remember a short pop and something being thrown on my face.

Several days later an elderly couple was driving by and happened to see a knapsack lying near the road. They stopped and discovered me. For the next seven years I lived with them. They often talked about the mysterious fire that took the lives of that nice couple and how nobody noticed me lying in the tall grass nearby. Since they were childless, they adopted me and I became their care giver. When they passed, I inherited their small farm, house, belongings and insurance, which was a substantial amount.

I can remember, at their funeral Mrs. Rose Fletcher mentioning we had the same name and I was a very fortunate lady.

CHAPTER 16

The Demolition of Pearl's Beauty Shop

Tom Malone had wasted no time in contacting the proper authorities to begin clearing the way for the brand new highway. In fact he was hoping it would encourage Rose to finally relinquish her deed for The Shady Rest Funeral Home. Charlie, Maudelle's husband, didn't care for the idea that Pearl was going to be living with them for a while, but he cooled down after Maudelle promised to take him gambling in Biloxi two times a week.

Pearl had managed with her son Timmy, to move everything worthwhile out the night before. Bubba Cuevas stopped by to help for an hour or two, but he left and joined all the other volunteers to look for Dr. Horatio Banks, Aunt Jewels and Maggie May, the dog.

You should have seen the equipment Tom Malone had brought in. Rose Fletcher stood on the sidelines and said it reminded her of the television show, *Extreme Makeover*.

After the machines had gouged and stripped the back part of the house, another bulldozer came in and starting tearing up the linoleum covered floor. Just as quickly as the operator had placed the huge metal pointed blades in the earth, lifted it up and dumped it to the side, he stopped. "Mr. Malone?" he yelled.

"Yeah, what is it?" Tom answered.

"You might want to see this."

"Why, what did you do, break a water or a gas main?"

"Nope. Looks like bones to me. Human bones. Somebody was buried underneath the floor in the back room."

Rose Fletcher smiled. "Well now Tom, you might be happy I haven't signed those papers....yet!"

CHAPTER 17

Sheriff Jim Travis and Bea Winslow

"Hello?"

"Bea, Jim here. Say you had better meet me at Pearl's Beauty Shop." "Why? You need help curling your hair?"

"No, Tom Malone is tearing down the place and a bulldozer just dug up some human bones."

"I'm on my way!"

As Bea pulled up behind Jim's jeep, she saw Pearl and Maudelle standing off to the side. "Well now ladies, what's been going on lately?"

"Bea," stated Pearl, "I was just telling the Sheriff, I didn't know anything about any body buried under my house!"

"How about you Maudelle? Do you recall anything happening to anybody?"

"No, not right off."

"All right ladies," said Sheriff Travis, "we're going to wait for Dr. Nathan Tate from New Orleans to arrive. I've sealed off the area and the Deputies and I have strung yellow tape. Pearl, if you and Maudelle don't mind I would like you to stop by my office later on. There's no need for you to hang around here. I reckon you are plum tuckered out from moving everything."

"Well, thank God I had Timmy to help me."

"When did he arrive, Pearl?" Bea asked.

"It was yesterday," interrupted Maudelle. "I picked him up at the Greyhound Bus Station in Gulfport."

Pearl gave Maudelle a sharp look.

Out of the corner of Bea's eye, she caught the quick glance and inquired, "Is he staying long?"

Pearl let out a tiny giggle. "Oh you know my Timmy, Bea. He's in and out like a fiddler's bow. I was hoping that tearing down the shop was going to be the end of it, but now I don't know. Say, have you heard anything about your Aunt?"

"No ma'am, I haven't, but the Naval Investigation Service has their best men on the job. We have some clues."

"Well dear, I certainly hope you find her before Christmas and that little dog, too. My goodness Bea, all these shenanigans goin' on!"

"Sheriff," spoke Maudelle, "okay if I take Pearl back to the house?"

"Sure thing, Maudelle. Like I said before I'm waiting for Dr. Tate to arrive and later on you can bring your sister to my office."

As both of them shuffled toward Maudelle's car, Pearl quietly said, "all right Maudelle, why did you lie back there and say you picked up Timmy in Gulfport when we both know it was in Bay St. Louis?"

CHAPTER 18

Tommy Lockhart

Well it had finally happened. Tommy Lockhart finished college and received his double major degree in cosmetology and mortuary science. Not only did he excel in the classroom, but he received a perfect score for his National Certificate from the Conference of Funeral Board of Examiners! In fact, Rose and a group of both his and her friends attended his graduation and took him out for dinner and drinks later.

The next morning, when he awoke, he was shocked to look up and see his reflection in the mirrored ceiling!

A soft, sweet "yoohoo" was coming from the other side of the door. "Well, I must say, you are a sleepy head, but then we did party until the wee hours, didn't we?"

All Tommy could do was shake his numb head up and down, and mumble, "Yes."

"Now you get dressed. I've washed and pressed your shirt and even given you a new tie. Hurry up now, your breakfast is getting cold!"

Tommy was used to college girls, fraternity parties and an occasional beer at The Hole in One Bar on Cainey Creek Road. This was his first experience with a full, mature woman and he wasn't quite sure how to handle it! Of course being a gentleman, he wasn't going to kiss and tell. Not like that young guy on the television show. But it did raise a lot of questions. Seeing her everyday would somehow put a different view of things. He gazed about the spacious room with its canopied windows and tossed pillows placed on a velvet loveseat nestled underneath. Tucked in the corner stood a Chippendale table, complete with a miniature Tiffany lamp. To complete the illusion, soft music floated in from speakers cleverly disguise behind imitation palm trees.

"Oh sweetie!" She cooed, "hurry up now, I have a lot of errands to do!"

Yes, Tommy Lockhart had graduated....in more ways than one!

CHAPTER 19

Barry Luce, Naval Investigation Service, Bea Winslow and Sheriff Travis, Meet At The Sheriffs Office

"I called Ms. Winslow, Mr. Luce," spoke Sheriff Travis, "as soon as you notified me of your findings."

"Well people, I personally think there's a lot more to this than just your Aunt, Ms. Winslow, being kidnapped and them taking the dog also. The fact that Dr. Horatio Banks is missing too, leads me to believe somebody wanted his knowledge concerning the upcoming shuttle launch. You see he invented a small computer chip, which has to be manually inserted into the computerized mechanism. Now, I'm no rocket scientist, but that little gadget is mighty important and I'm sorry to say, we have unscrupulous people who would pay top dollar, in the millions for that knowledge."

"So, what you are saying, Mr. Luce," Bea replied, "is my Aunt Jewels was in the wrong place at the wrong time."

"Exactly. The minute we realized a switch had been made…"

"What do you mean by a switch?" Questioned the Sheriff.

The kidnappers apparently had planned this for some time. A man disguised as Dr. Horatio Banks was put in place, we estimate about a day before. They fingerprinted the real Dr. Banks and used his palm print and index finger to enter his secured office. Apparently they did not find what they were looking for."

"So," Bea began, "who was going to give the speech?"

"The fake one, Ms. Winslow; however, their cleverness backfired, so to speak, when their car had a blowout. Two of our units were following them. We quickly surrounded the vehicle and took the four men into custody."

"So Mr. Luce," Bea replied, "I take it your men took them to New Orleans to be incarcerated?"

"New Orleans? Ms. Winslow?"

"Yes sir, because it happened on Federal Property."

"Why yes, certainly. Also, in the car, one of my men found a remote device. They had sent a cryptic message to their partners who had the real Dr. Horatio Banks. Now think back to what the proprietors of Maggie May's Gift Shop told you."

"You mean about Aunt Jewels?" Bea asked.

"I certainly do ma'am. The men stated the sharp dresser went over to pet the dog. That had to be Dr. Banks and I believe he had the important small device on him and concealed it in the dog's blanket."

"Now I see what you're getting at," exclaimed Bea. "Aunt Jewels went back to retrieve her earring and possibly discovered that whatcha-ma-call-it."

"Absolutely!"

"Oh, my God!" Bea cried out loud. "If they find out...."

"I know what you're thinking and it's not good. I'm afraid I have some other bad news."

"What's that?" asked the Sheriff.

Dr. Luce furrowed his brow. "Seven years ago a house fire on Vancleave road, consumed a Darlene and Curtis Burras. Now Darlene was involved in a Federal scheme and was due to start serving her six-month jail term. She and Curtis Burras died in that fire. When forensics and DNA were performed on bone marrow, technicians confirmed her death...but not Curtis Burras."

"Mr. Luce," Sheriff Travis smiled, "I have something that you just might be interested in. Well, I don't have it yet, but it's coming soon, by Federal Express. A woman called me the other day and told me she was shipping me information on Curtis Burras."

"Wonderful!"

Bea sat there thinking. "Mr. Luce, did you know that Horatio Banks Jr.'s body washed up on the beach near Espy Avenue?"

"I heard about that, yes ma'am. I believe you handled that, didn't you Sheriff?"

"Yes sir, and I called Dr. Nathan Tate, the New Orleans Coroner."

"Wasn't somebody else involved, a Betsy......"

"Betsy Malone Prender," Bea began, "our part-time coroner for Lafouchfeye County. Why?"

"Oh nothing....I was just looking over the papers concerning his father. Well, thank you both for this meeting. I'll get with you later and let you know how the investigation is coming. I have another meeting I have to attend. Bye now."

"Thank you Mr. Luce and see you later!" replied the Sheriff. After Mr. Luce had left the room, the Sheriff notice Bea was watching him getting into his car. "Okay Bea, I know that look. I've seen it before. What's wrong?"

CHAPTER 20

Rose and Maudelle's Conversation at The Shady Rest Funeral Home

"Thank you Ms. Rose for inviting me along last night to celebrate Tommy's graduation," exclaimed Maudelle.

"Well my dear," Rose smiled, "I know you don't have much time for frivolous activity, so I thought a good time should be had by all!"

"Did you and Mr. Fletcher dance much?"

"Goodness, yes! We won several dance contests over in New Orleans. I love to dance and Tommy is such an excellent fox-trot partner."

"Did you happen to catch Bubba Cuevas dancing with Cyrus Dedeaux's ex-wife?"

"I sure did. She has slimmed down since their divorce. Maudelle, are you still seeing Cyrus?"

"Why Rose, whatever do you mean?"

"Oh my dear, come on now, I wasn't born yesterday. Why I have known about you and Cyrus Dedeaux since before he went to prison. In fact, you two were here that night my husband, Horace was killed."

"How would you know that...unless you were here also?" Maudelle questioned.

"Let's just say a little bird told me."

"Well, for your information, I don't see Cyrus anymore. As a matter of fact, I do believe he's taken up with a woman who recently moved into the old Barber place."

"You mean Jeannie Rose?"

"Is that her name?" Maudelle replied, blinking her eyes.

"Yes, and I happen to know her circumstances also. But you have work to do and so have I, so we'll have to continue our chat another time. Oh yes, Maudelle, please clean up the Lincoln Parlor extra special. We're having Horatio Banks, Jr.'s services in there tomorrow!"

CHAPTER 21

Crissy Dubois Malone

She hadn't heard from her husband Tom for a week now and that was very unusual. Of course she herself had been working long, tedious hours on that tax evasion case. Her firm of Holloway, Dubois and Ross had just received pertinent documents from the office of Lawton, Coast and Dunlap, located in the town of Lumberton, Mississippi. If it weren't for a very important meeting tomorrow, Crissy would have jumped into her Volvo and headed towards Lafouchfeye County. Oh well, she thought, he's probably up to his neck in paperwork or dirt. In fact he made it quite clear, he wouldn't have time for her.

As she pushed papers around on her desk, she thought how differently she and her cousin Darlene Dubois Burras' lives had turned out. Crissy had a loving husband, a successful career, a beautiful house and sheer happiness. Whereas Darlene fell in love with a schemer, chiseler, and womanizer and in the end, he had convinced Darlene to become an accomplice in his dirty business.

Crissy was very sad to hear of their deaths. Of course having them as friends in the beginning was wonderful! They had enjoyed some good times together.

Crissy and Darlene were more like sisters than cousins and had been together constantly, ever since kindergarten. In high school, it was Darlene who saved Crissy's life that cold February night when she wrecked her car. Crissy would have bled to death if it weren't for Darlene's quick action in making a tourniquet.

When Darlene met Curtis, through Tom, Crissy was so pleased. Tom had expressed his approval, also.

Naturally, when that terrible disaster happened, Crissy and Tom were questioned about Darlene and Curtis' activities. Tom was quite protective of her and she appreciated that.

As she propped up her chin between her two hands, she soulfully thought I wonder what he's doing right now?

She didn't have to wonder long at all, because the mute cell phone chimed a little tune. Her blue eyes became bright and wide grin produced dimples in both cheeks, when she looked at the number. It wasn't Tom's. "Darling, I thought you'd never call……"

CHAPTER 22

Gerald Sheppard also known as Curtis Burras Talks With Tom Malone

"Hello?"

"Where in the hell have you been?" Gerald demanded.

"Busy, man…just busy."

Tom snickered into the phone. "The plan is on hold…for now."

"What? Hey….I have investors and bank officials screaming at me for repayment. What the hell are you talking about…on hold?"

"We found some bones."

There was a pause, and then a deep drawn out breath. "What bones?"

"Well, it seems somebody died about twenty-twenty-five years ago and their bones were buried under Pearl's closet floor."

"So……, what now?"

"Sheriff Travis and Dr. Nathan Tate…"

"The Coroner from New Orleans?"

"The one and only."

"Why didn't Travis get your Aunt Betsy?"

"She's out of town."

"So how long do you think the delay will be? Did Rose Fletcher sell?"

"Answer to the first question is, I don't know. Answer to the second question, and you're not going to like it, but no."

"Look Malone, we need that land and we need it now! The government land borders it. That bill is coming up and my sources in Washington D.C. want it covered! You understand?"

"I get the picture….how's your girlfriend?" Tom asked.

"She's fine. How's your wife?" Gerald replied.

"Crissy's very busy. I take it Dr. Banks' disappearance has something to do with it also?"

Gerald laughed. "You got that right…doesn't hurt to have a little leverage."

"Okay, how does that P.I.'s Aunt and that dog fit in?"

"They just happened along, that's all."

"What's going to happen them?" Tom asked.

"When everything is settled…accidents do happen, you know. Malone, hurry things up, the folks up here in Washington D.C. have extended this operation for a few days, but they want it done by Christmas. Me and the doll have plans to go to Aspen…so don't fail me buddy."

"No problem Burras, I mean Sheppard…no problem at all," were Tom's last words, as he closed his cell phone.

"Sweetie," she whispered, "who was that, that upset you so?"

"No one for your little head to worry about," and then Tom rolled over on his back. "Man, I do like this mirror ceiling!"

CHAPTER 23

Horatio Bank Jr.'s Funeral

The turnout for Horatio Bank Jr's funeral didn't surprise Bea at all. She knew because of his father, Dr. Horatio Banks Sr. and the law firm that Horatio Jr. worked for Holloway, Dubois and Ross would be sure that he was properly recognized. What did shock her was the bronze urn sitting on the marble pedestal, which contained his ashes. She remembered he always admired the lavish funeral processions through the French Quarter, with the Jazz Society Band playing, "When The Saints Come Marching In", Second-lining and weaving their way down Bourbon Street. Now that was his kind of funeral! She thought, so why the ashes? While she waited for Sheriff Jim Travis to arrive, she watched the people file past the flowers and photographs that depicted Horatio's life achievements. Hugging the back wall was a young lady, about twenty-five, quietly weeping. Bea meandered over to her. "Excuse me ma'am," she asked, "did you know the deceased?"

She was wearing a large black hat with a single pink rose tucked neatly in the brim. As she raised her head, she replied, "Excuse me?"

Bea repeated the question. "I asked, did you know the deceased?"

"Why yes, yes, I did. I worked for him. My name is Tina Favre. This is so tragic. I really can't believe he's gone. The help for humanity this man performed was just astonishing. You know, he was always for the underdog. Why just last month he managed to set a man free who had been in jail for seven years! Can you imagine being locked up for a crime you didn't commit? I am going to miss him so much!"

"Ms. Favre," began Bea, "do you live around here?"

"I'm surprised you haven't asked me if I know Brett."

"Brett?" Bea inquired.

"You know, Brett Favre, from Kiln, Mississippi."

"Oh yes, the football Quarterback. Well, do you?"

"We're not closely related. He's a distant cousin."

"I see," Bea smiled.

Ms. Favre dabbed her eyes with a well-used tissue. "Did you know Horatio, I mean Mr. Banks?"

"I went to school with him."

"Really!"

"Yes, really."

"And you are?" Ms. Favre asked.

"I'm sorry, my name is Bea Winslow. I'm a Private Investigator."

"It's very nice to meet you, Ms. Winslow."

"I take it," asked Bea, "you were on more friendly terms with Mr. Banks, Jr., than just his secretary."

Ms. Farve blushed. "Yes, we were special friends. At one time Horatio had asked me to marry him. Oh, how foolish I was then. Now…, I wish I had. Do you realize Ms. Winslow, Horatio was the most honest person I have ever met. He absolutely adored his father and mother. Isn't it just terrible that his father is missing?"

"Yes…Ms. Favre, it is," Bea agreed.

"And he just talked to him the other day."

"Talked to who, Ms. Favre?"

Tina Favre let out a suppressed giggle, "Why his father, Dr. Banks, of course, Ms. Winslow. It was so funny. Horatio kept repeating his father's message out loud. 'Dog gone……dog gone….Christmas'."

"What does that mean?" Bea inquired.

"I certainly don't know Ms. Winslow," as Tina leaned in towards Bea's shoulder. "And another thing, Horatio and I both loved to watch the colorful send-offs of the traditional New Orleans funerals. I'll never understand why Horatio's mother consented to his cremation!"

Immediately Bea turned her entire body toward Ms. Favre and faced her.

"Did I say something?" Ms. Favre questioned.

"Excuse me please, Ms. Favre. Sheriff Travis has just arrived and I must see if any progress has been made in finding my Aunt Jewels."

CHAPTER 24

Maudelle Calls Deputy Paulie

"Deputy Paulie, this is Maudelle Perkins. I was wondering if you could stop by and help me get Charlie in the car. I promised him a ride in the country."

"Sure thing Maudelle. As soon as Sheriff Travis returns from Mr. Banks' funeral services."

"I just couldn't make it," Maudelle sighed. "Rose had me clean the Lincoln parlor extra special."

"I know how you feel. Say, how's your sister doin' and her son Timmy?"

"They're okay. Still a little shocked about livin' over a corpse for over twenty years!"

"Yeah, that was somethin' all right. So far we haven't gotten any results back, but I did hear somethin' about the new highway."

"What was that?"

"Well, Maudelle, it seems there's a lot of commotion up in D.C. Look, I gotta go. I'll be there as soon as Sheriff Travis drives up."

"Thanks, Deputy Paulie, see you soon."

CHAPTER 25

Dr. Nathan Tate, Sheriff Travis and Bea At Dr. Tate's New Orleans Office

While grasping the doctor's hand like the handle of water pump, the Sheriff replied, "Thank you, thank you, Nathan, for making time to see us."

"I can tell when there's a wee bit of urgency in your voice Jim. Is something the matter?"

"Nathan, remember when they discovered that body that washed up on Espy Avenue?"

"Yes, you called me and I came over. Just like I usually do. Why?"

"Dr. Tate," Bea cut in, "could we see the documents concerning Horatio Banks, Jr.?"

"Certainly, but I still don't understand...."

"Dr. Tate," smiled Bea, "they, Rose Fletcher and The Shady Rest Funeral Home had his services earlier today. He was cremated."

"Cremated?"

"That's right. Now I went to school with Horatio and while I was at the Funeral Home, I met his secretary, Tina Favre. I can remember Horatio loving the New Orleans way of celebrating death......marching s-l-o-w-l-y with a parade thru the St. Louis Cemeteries. They go to the St. Louis Cemeteries marching very slowly, and then they return marching more quickly. The most familiar song is *"Just a Closer Walk With Thee."* Well, his secretary, at one time, was almost his wife, and she also recalled his desire for that kind of funeral."

"So, Ms. Winslow, why the interest?"

"Ms. Favre told me that Horatio's mother ordered his cremation. That's impossible, Dr. Tate. Mrs. Horatio Banks has been dead almost a year!"

"Well now, I have all the paperwork concerning this case in my office, so let's give a look-see."

"Do you remember her, Nathan? You know, identifying her son's body?" asked Sheriff Travis.

Neat little piles of paperwork were stacked in rows of threes across his desk. Now, Dr. Tate systematically thumbed through the uppermost three-stack. "I was going over my notes on this particular case the other night. It fascinated me. Of course, the cadaver had water in his lungs, but he didn't drown. No, he was shot in the chest, and then dumped out in the Gulf. He had been dead for about three days. The creatures of the sea had...."

"Please sir," choked the Sheriff, "please, if you don't mind."

"No problem, Jim. Oh, here we are. According to these release papers, his mother signed right here. As I recall, she was a portly woman."

"About Ms. Rose Fletcher's size?" quizzed the Sheriff.

"Whose signature is this?" questioned Bea.

"The witness," answered Dr. Tate. "That's one of the morticians that works for Rose Fletcher. Bubba Cuevas. Sometimes he moonlights and helps me out. Good man, Bubba. Yes Jim, I'd say she was about Rose Fletcher's size."

Bea gave the Sheriff a jab. "Well, at least they're not hard to find."

"So," Dr. Tate replied, while peering over his wire-frame glasses, "what I think you're saying is, you don't believe that Horatio Banks, Jr. is dead....agreed?"

"That's right Nathan," nodded the Sheriff. "Someone else's ashes are in that urn."

"Now Jim," Dr. Tate continued, while pointing again to Horatio Banks, Jr.'s papers, "do you think he faked his own death?"

"Personally, Dr. Tate," Jim replied, "I think someone wants us to think he's dead. No sir, I don't think he faked it."

"Okay, Dr. Tate, let's change the subject a minute. How about those bones that were found buried underneath Pearl's back room?"

Pushing around some more papers, Dr. Tate brought up a manila folder, marked J.B. or J.F. "They're a man's bones, about twenty-five years of age. I'd estimate. He was hit on the back of his head, probably with a blunt instrument, like a large hammer. When I examined where the body had been found, I discovered a ring."

"What kind of ring?" asked Bea.

"A black onyx with the initials J.B. or it could be an F."

"Who all was there at the time of your discovery?" probed the Sheriff.

"Well now, let's see. Tom Malone, but he just stood on the sidelines. Bubba was there. In fact he helped me dig. Of course, Pearl, Timmy, Maudelle and Rose were sitting in the white wicker rockers on the porch of The Shady Rest Funeral Home."

"Well, sir," Jim replied, "did you know that Horatio Banks, Jr. was the lawyer that released Cyrus Dedeaux?"

"I didn't realize it until I read about it in the newspaper. Maybe Jim, there's a connection. I don't mind telling you, I do not like being wrong."

"I understand and thanks a lot Nathan, for all your time and trouble," replied Jim.

"Ms. Winslow, have you heard any news about your Aunt?" asked the Doctor.

"No sir, but the Naval Investigative Service is working diligently on it."

"Who's heading up the case?" he asked.

"The name is Luce, Barry Luce," Bea answered.

"I don't recall that name. Maybe he's out of Washington, D.C. Y'all be careful driving back now, and Jim, keep me informed."

"Dr. Tate." Bea questioned, if you judged those bones to be that of a twenty-five year old man, then if he would have lived, he would be......"

"Around sixty to sixty-five," interrupted Dr. Tate. "Like I said, keep me informed."

"Sure thing Nathan, sure thing," Jim replied, while throwing him a half salute. Glancing over in Bea's direction, he rolled his eyes. "Oh, oh, you have that look again!"

CHAPTER 26

Captain Eric VonBoatner Visits Bea

As the Sheriff and Bea rounded the last turn in his jeep and headed for Aunt Jewel's and Bea's house, she spied Captain VonBoatner's Nissan in the driveway.

"Jim, look, Captain Eric is at our house….waiting."

He was pacing back and forth beside his car. After they got out of the jeep, Eric quickly approached and asked, "Have you heard anything?"

"No sir, no word yet. Now don't you fret. We are going to find her," Bea assured him. "It's just we haven't gotten a good lead…yet."

"We did make some headway however," replied Sheriff Travis.

"In what?" Eric asked.

"Well, for one, the body that washed up on the shore was not Horatio Banks, Jr. and the twenty-five year old corpse buried under Pearl's Beauty Shop had a ring with the initials J.B.," revealed the Sheriff.

"Or," Bea interrupted, "Dr. Tate said the initial could be an F."

"It just boggles my mind as to why they took Julia and that dog!" Eric exclaimed.

"I know you're upset and I'm also concerned about Aunt Jewels, Eric." Bea said while squeezing his shoulder, "but like Jim said before, we have to keep cool heads."

CHAPTER 27

Tom Malone's Visitor at the Motel

He had just received his pizza, coke and cinnamon sticks, when the quick knock on his motel door startled him. Pushing aside the curtain, he was surprised at who he saw. "Well, now, what brings you way out here at the edge of town?"

"To see you, Tom Malone. You can only be here for one reason. Money. No use denying it because your whole life has been a quest for money and more money, plus women."

"Would you like to come in and share some pizza with me? Tom smiled. "However honey, I do have an important engagement and I will have to leave soon."

"Thanks, but no thanks."

"Does anybody know……"

"That I'm in town?" Not that I know of. I didn't come to visit and chit chat. I came to see you."

Grabbing a big slice of pizza and stuffing it in his mouth, his words were garbled. "So……, you don't know what we've found under the beauty shop."

"No and I don't care. Like I said…"

"Yeah, honey, I know. It's me, all me."

Mae Beth stepped closer to him. "My momma and Aunt Maudelle woulda killed you if they knew you the way I know you."

He laughed! "But you didn't tell them, so where does that leave us now?"

"Tom Malone, don't play games with me!"

"Look Mae Beth, I'm not as bad as you want to believe. Sure, we had fun for awhile, but that was a long time ago. As far as the business dealings with your momma, now she is getting a fair price for that property."

Mae Beth stood there, with her arms crossed. "My husband Chester's kinfolk gave me the paperwork which absolutely shows where the government land begins and ends and it ain't showin' on none of your plans!"

Tom quickly pulled Mae Beth against his chest. "Look honey, I have to close this deal before Christmas and that means I don't have time to argue with the likes of you. So, you might as well go back to where you came from!"

"We'll see about that!" Mae Beth yelled and stomped out the door. A second later, Tom's cell phone rang. "Hello? Oh hi…no.. Just ordering a pizza. Care to join me? Wait a minute, I have a better idea. That's right. I'm a sucker for that mirrored ceiling!"

CHAPTER 28

At the Hideaway on Highway 603

As Meathead shoved Mousy's shoulder, he snickered. "How's that old broad doin'?"

"She's still knocked out. Hey, Meathead, have you heard from anybody on that little contraption?"

"You mean this here cell phone?"

"Yeah."

"Sure have. They're gonna be bringin' that doc's kid out here pretty soon."

"I thought he was dead!"

"That was the whole idea Mousy. For everybody to think he was dead."

"Well….why ain't he dead, then?"

"Because lunkhead, he's a lawyer and we may need him."

"Ohhhhhhh…, I see….., no Meathead, I don't see."

"Look Mousy, maybe afterwards when we don't need the guys brains anymore, well you know. We can dump him. Wait a minute. Did you hear somethin'?"

Mousy became very quiet. "I think the old girl is stirring around," he whispered, "I'll go check on her." As he unlatched the bolt, he heard Maggie May growling from the other side of the door and changed his mind. Re-latching the bolt, he stepped back and told Meathead, "She's okay."

CHAPTER 29

Jeannie Rose, Sheriff Travis and Bea Winslow

As Sheriff Travis drove his jeep past the broken mesh wire gate and headed towards the front porch, Bea replied, "The place looks deserted Jim."

"Jeannie Rose said to meet her at the old Barber house and this is it."

"There she is Jim, there, in the shadows, by the porch glider."

"Thank you for meeting me here, Sheriff Travis," smiled Jeannie.

"I hope you didn't mind, I invited Ms. Bea Winslow along, also."

"I know who you are, Ms. Winslow, you're that Private Investigator."

"That's correct Jeannie."

"Well now," Jeannie gestured with her hand, "let's go inside and sit down. We have lots to talk about!"

With the moonlight shining down on them, they filed one by one inside the house, through the rusted screened door. "This way," Jeannie Rose replied, leading the way into the dimly lit living room. She had propped up several flashlights, illuminating spots on the dusty ceiling. Over two large chairs and a loveseat she had placed some white sheets. "We can sit here."

"Now, just what is it you have to show us?" Bea asked.

"All I know is, Curtis Burras is alive and he didn't die in that fire. He tried to kill me, but he goofed. There's a big deal doing down about this land deal for the highway. Tom Malone is in charge of it. I've been seeing him for about five months now."

"Jeannie," questioned the Sheriff, "you said you were going to mail me some information. Did you do it?"

"No, I thought better of it and decided we should meet. Here are the documents I have accumulated. I hope it helps."

Sheriff Travis and Bea began pouring out the contents of the manila envelope atop of the trunk like coffee table. Stapled together were pictures, receipts, passport photos of Curtis and Darlene Burras, and government letterhead from Washington, D.C. and surrounding areas.

As Jeannie Rose pointed to Curtis Burras' picture, she blurted, "I know that Curtis is behind the disappearance of Dr. Banks too. Also I saw Bubba Cuevas load up his fishing boat with a large bundle a few days ago. It could have been that body that washed up, Sheriff."

"Just what do you know about that?" Asked the Sheriff.

"I went to Tommy Lockhart's graduation party that Ms. Rose Fletcher gave at the pavilion by the Bay and Bubba Cuevas was drunk and shooting off his mouth about things."

"What things?" Bea asked.

"Oh....like...he's going to get a bigger boat, leave the Bay and fish off the Jamaican coastline."

As Bea was separating some more papers, her eye caught the name on a piece of paper from Stennis Space Center. "Well, well. Would you look at this Jim?"

He stopped and looked up, asking, "What?"

"Look at the name on this letterhead and then scan down to the signature on the right side."

"Well, I'll be."

Jeannie Rose's eyes lit up. "Have you found something useful?"

"I don't know if it's useful, but it's sure interesting. You have a letter with Dr. Horatio Banks' name and title at the top, but the signature is signed by Dr. Barry Luce, PhD.," smiled Bea. "I knew there was something about that man! Jim, Barry Luce worked in Washington D.C. with The Federal Bureau of Investigation, when I was there. Only his name wasn't Barry then. It was Abner Luce. When we get back home, I'm e-mailing my friend Mac Tavis."

Rubbing the back of his neck, Jim replied, "Thought he retired?"

"Yes, he did, but he moonlights also. Now listen Jim, we can't tip our hand that we know about Luce's involvement," and they both looked at Jeannie Rose.

She nodded her head in agreement. "You can count on me not to tell anybody!"

Unanimously, the Sheriff and Bea sighed, "We hope so, we certainly hope so!"

CHAPTER 30

Maudelle and Charlie

"Thanks a lot Deputy Paulie," smiled Maudelle. "I really do appreciate you helpin' me get Charlie in the front seat."

"No problem Mrs. Perkins. I know he'll enjoy the ride."

After Maudelle had driven down Beach Drive Boulevard a ways, Charlie mumbled, "okay, there's gotta be a reason why you're doin' this, so, what is it?"

"There's no particular reason Charlie, I just figured you hadn't been out of the house in awhile and you would enjoy the outing."

"You must want somethin'."

"No…nothing. You haven't complained that much about Pearl and Timmy being there either."

"Well, you know I don't like it. It interferes with our privacy!"

"What privacy, Charlie? You're downstairs and I'm upstairs with Pearl and Timmy."

"You know what I mean."

"Oh….that. Well, some things just have to work themselves out, that's all. Here we are. Look at that view. Isn't it gorgeous?"

"Yeah, it's pretty all right. You plannin' on dumpin' me here Maudelle?"

Maudelle turned toward him and stared. "No, Charlie, I don't plan on dumpin' you out here on the sand. Remember when we used to come here with a bottle of wine and a blanket. Just lie in each others arms and look up at the stars?"

"Yeah,..those were good times. Then the next thing I know, you up and left."

"I was young, Charlie. I didn't know I had a good thing when I had it. I came back didn't I?"

"Yeah, then you started messin' around with that Cyrus dude."

"Why did you come down to the funeral parlor, Charlie?"

"I don't know...jealous, I guess. Hey, does Rose still have that mirrored ceiling?"

"I wish I knew who whacked you across the back. How come you know about the mirrored ceiling Charlie?"

"When Horace was alive, he showed it to me one time. He said one of his customers wanted mirrors put on the ceiling, just in case the deceased woke up."

"How positively gross Charlie. I believe Horace was a sick man. You know I was talking to Rose the other day and she said she was at the funeral home seven years ago, when Horace was killed."

"No kiddin', Maudelle. Maybe she was the one that tried to split me in half. I sure wish I knew! They really did a number on me! Hey, look, we may have company."

"Where?" Maudelle asked.

"Right over there. See that car creeping along the road? Did you mention to anybody we were comin' out here?"

"Only Deputy Paulie."

"That's not his patrol car. Maybe we'd better start back home."

"If you want, Charlie, if you want. Hand me your little cell phone and I'll call Deputy Paulie to meet us at the house."

CHAPTER 31

Sheriff Travis and Bea Winslow Pick Up The Old Car

While they drove back from the old Barber place, Sheriff Travis glanced over at Bea and uttered, "Go ahead, and say it."

"Say what, Jim?"

"You were right about the Luce fella."

"Jim, I didn't know I was right, I just had a hunch. I don't know, there was something about his mannerisms, his attitude."

"Well, how come I don't see those things, Bea?"

"Jim, you notice lots of things. Remember, it was you who identified the body that washed up as Banks, Jr. You mentioned Bubba Cuevas was with you that day."

"Yeah, and I was wrong."

"Listen Jim, I would have thought the same thing. You had his wallet and other identification. And besides, Bubba was there."

"What do you want to do, now?" asked Jim.

"We still have time to pick up that old car Aunt Jewels won."

"Okay, we're on our way! Excuse me Bea, but do you know where it's at?"

"Got the directions right here, partner!"

Thirty minutes later, Jim parked the jeep in back of the Bay Town Bed and Breakfast Inn. There in the side drive sat the 1927 Model T. Ford.

From the narrow back porch, came the sound of a gravelly, raspy voice, "The Ford's a beauty isn't it?"

"Good evening sir. This is Sheriff Jim Travis and I'm Bea Winslow. My Aunt, Mrs. Julia McKenna won this car several months ago."

"I know, Ms. Winslow. My name is Amos Seals. I'm the one who called," and then he coughed, repeatedly.

As Bea nonchalantly approached him, she studied his whiskered face and frayed suspenders and then extended her hand. "Very happy to meet you Mr. Seals. Can I drive it home?"

"Sure, little lady, no problem, she's all gassed up."

"Does my Aunt need any papers or bill of sale?"

"Naw……, not right now. Have you found her?"

"My Aunt? No….not yet, Mr. Seals."

"What's this world comin' to? A nice lady like that and a poor defenseless little dog. Just snatched right out from under her friends' nose! And that good Doctor too!"

"We'll find them Mr. Seals," Sheriff Travis replied. "We have several good leads!"

"If I can be of any more help to you Sheriff…..Ms. Winslow, don't you hesitate to come by. I'm always here. I'm the handyman around the place, you know."

"I'll remember that Mr. Seals. Bye now."

Jim stopped, then asked, "Are you really going to drive this thing home Bea?"

Bea turned sharply. "Do you want to?"

Jim threw up his hands in protest and laughed. "No, I'll follow you, though."

"I was planning on that," Bea grinned.

After opening the small door, she flashed her penlight towards the ignition and across the floorboards. Something speckled was down there. "Jim, give me your large flashlight, please."

"What is it?" he asked.

After he unhooked his flashlight from his belt and gave it to her, she began examining the floorboards closer. Bea started nodding her head. "Jim, there's dried blood on the front passenger side."

Suddenly, once more Mr. Seal's coughing and gruff voice pierced the silence. "Anything wrong little lady?"

Rising up, Bea hit her head on the steering wheel! "Oh!"

"I said, anything wrong?"

"No…no sir, I dropped my penlight and was searching for it. We're ready to leave now. Thanks, though! Are you ready to roll, Jim?"

"Ready when you are, Bea."

"See you later, Mr. Seals and thanks again."

CHAPTER 32

Christmas Is Five Days Away Deputy Paulie Helps Maudelle and Charlie

"Deputy Paulie here. Oh, hi there…what's up? No, Maudelle, no problem at all. Deputy Taylor is here. Seems the Sheriff and Bea are finally pickin' up that car Aunt Jewels won. Where are you? Yeah,.right I'll meet you at y'alls house."

Propping his feet up on the end of the desk, Deputy Taylor asked, "Who was that?"

"Maudelle Perkins. I helped her get her husband Charlie in the car about an hour ago. She can't do it by herself."

"Yeah……, I remember. That's the guy who got whacked inside the funeral home seven years ago. Ya know, I never quite figured that one out. His wife is makin' out with that creepy mortician and he comes sneakin' around the side entrance, gets whacked…"

Deputy Paulie snickered. "You already said that Taylor."

"Okay, okay…so I did, didn't I, but then Mr. Fletcher was dead and I guess Maudelle Perkins and Cyrus Dedeaux put Charlie in his car and Maudelle drives him home."

"Just what point are you tryin' to make, Taylor?"

"They let Cyrus Dedeaux go free, so who killed Horace Fletcher? Now we received the fax from Dr. Tate, tellin' us that body wasn't Horatio Banks, Jr.'s body. Poor Mrs. McKenna and that pooch got lifted. I called my ma in Poughkeepsie and told her I'd be home for Christmas. Now…I'm not so sure, ya know what I mean?"

"Yeah Taylor, don't worry. Sheriff Travis will let you off for Christmas. It's only five days away. Look, hold down the fort. I'll be right back."

"Where ya goin'? You know….if the Sheriff should ask when he gets back."

"I told ya. I'm helpin' Maudelle get Charlie in their house."

"Oh…yeah…now I remember."

Deputy Paulie hadn't taken three steps outside the Sheriff's office and towards his car, when he was tapped on his shoulder, from behind.

CHAPTER 33

Meathead Gets An Important Phone Call

Things were finally quiet in the three room shack, located off the dusty dirt road, north of Highway 603. The two prisoners and the dog were snoozing like babies. Even Mousy had decided to take a short forty winks. Meathead rested his heavy frame on two legs of the chair he was perched in. Suddenly a small jingle caused him to sit upright. "Hello? Yeah, everything is quiet…now. No, they're okay. No, I haven't found it and I don't know if he's got it. Look boss, I'm keepin' my end of this bargain. I got the Doc and even an old lady and a dog. Why, I don't know. They haven't brought the Doc's son out here yet. What'ya mean you don't know when that's gonna happen? I can't stay out here forever! Hey……I hear a truck comin'." Meathead got up and shuffled over to the burlap covered window. "Yeah……it's that broad……gosh I didn't know she was in on it too! She's got the Doc's son! Okay then, I'll talk at you later. Don't worry boss, you can count on me!"

CHAPTER 34

Mr. Abner Bartholomew (Barry) Luce

He had used his position of authority very, very well, he thought. Having once worked with The Federal Bureau of Investigation, he was aware of that Private Investigator, Bea Winslow and her bag of tricks. Yes, Barry Luce had extremely covered his bases and tracks. Of course, he realized his inside person was to be complimented also. He couldn't have done it without her. After all she was a pillar in the small community of Lafouchfeye County and had connections. Now it was all coming together. He felt assured that Meathead and Mousy had their end under control. She had phoned him personally and told him that she would be taking the Doc's son out to the hideaway.

Now as Barry waited for Curtis Burras (also known as Gerald Sheppard) to meet him at an abandon boat ramp behind the vacant summer home on North Beach, he was quite pleased. Seven years he had patiently waited for his reward. He chuckled quietly to himself when he thought about Bea Winslow's old Aunt. She was a meddlesome biddy. But, she and that dog would soon be out of the picture. He had reprimanded Meathead for letting the good Doctor pet that animal in the first place. Then when Meathead said he thought the old gal recognized the Doctor, well, that settled it. She and the dog would have to be 'detained' as he put it.

Just then a car passed him by, and then did a half donut in the middle of the dark road. As it slowly crept up beside him, he could tell it was Burras, but he also noticed a small sedan parked partially on the sand about five hundred yards away and wondered who it belonged to.

CHAPTER 35

Pearl Rooster and Rose Fletcher

"It's been a long time since we've sat down and had tea, Pearl," Rose smiled.

"But understandable," replied Pearl. "When there's nobody to depend on but yourself, sometimes you have to work harder."

"Don't I realize that now, since my Horace has been gone these past seven years. I certainly didn't comprehend what all that man did with this place."

"It was nice of you to take in Cyrus. You know, let him have his old job back."

"He's a good mortician, Pearl! Besides, he didn't kill Horace."

"Well, I know he was found innocent by his lawyer, Horatio Banks, Jr."

"No Pearl, I mean Cyrus didn't kill Horace in the first place."

"I don't understand Rose."

"I was here that evening with Horace and......I saw you and Bubba Cuevas."

Pearl's eyes grew wider and wider. "Whatever are you talkin' about?" Bubba Cuevas and me? Never!"

Rose let out a hearty laugh. "Pearl, honey, this is a small county and, well, I saw what I saw!"

"Are you suggestion, maybe me or Bubba killed your husband Horace?"

"Now honey, don't get me wrong, I didn't see the actual killing part, but I did see you and Bubba Cuevas in the parlor room....with the mirror ceiling."

Pearl stood up quickly. "Well, Rose Fletcher, if it was so important, why didn't you bring it out at Cyrus Dedeaux's trial? I'll tell you why you didn't! Because it didn't happen.....that way......, that way at all!"

Rose retaliated. "And another thing Pearl, I don't think I'm selling to Tom Malone! I've been hearing some conflicting stories about him and this so called highway! I have friends in Washington D.C. and they have been very interested in the land dealing down here. Especially since it borders around the Stennis Space Center!"

Pearl glanced across the entire room, until her eyes settled on the brass urn sitting in the middle of Rose Fletchers fireplace. Picking up her purse, Pearl turned and started for the door, and then stopped. Slowly she pivoted and pointed her index finger towards the urn encasement. "Horace Fletcher," Pearl stuttered, "you married a witch! Don't bother showing me the door, Rose, I know my way out!"

CHAPTER 36

Dr. Nathan Tate Confers With Sheriff Travis and Bea Winslow

Sheriff Travis was elated when Bea answered the phone. "Good Bea, I caught you home!"

"Jim, you sound out of breath. What on earth is the matter?"

"Look, Dr. Tate is coming to my office in about thirty minutes. Can you come over?"

Bea hesitated a bit. "Jim, he hasn't received any bad news about…."

"No, no, nothing like that. It's something else. Something that will tee-totally surprise you!"

"See you in a few minutes, Jim."

He let out a heavy sigh, after hanging up the phone. Ever since then, who-ever that woman was and Bubba Cuevas played a fast one on Dr. Tate, Jim could tell the good doctor was going to get to the bottom of the whole scheme. He had told him earlier in a phone conversation and e-mail that he, Dr. Tate had personally talked to Bubba Cuevas asking about the woman who posed as Horatio Banks, Jr.'s mother. Naturally he swore on a stack of Bibles that he, Bubba Cuevas didn't know anything about a scheme to make millions off a land deal! Bubba Cuevas even had an alibi for later on that very afternoon, say-ing he was on a picnic with Jeannie Rose at Ghost Bayou Lake, at the other side of the entrance to Buccaneer Park.

Almost twenty minutes later, both Dr. Tate and Bea arrived at the Sheriff's office. The minute they sat down around the table, Dr. Tate began.

"Ms. Winslow, you were correct about the Barry Luce fella. Sure, he still is an FBI Agent, well, sort of. He's on probation at present. You'll probably get the same information from your source, Tavis. No, I have found out some startling news about Horace Fletcher. A body was cremated, but I don't believe it was his."

Sheriff Travis almost slipped off his chair. "What?"

"Why would you think that?" Bea asked. "Cyrus Dedeaux was blamed and convicted for his murder."

"And Horatio Banks, Jr., his lawyer, got him out seven years later. No, if that woman and Bubba Cuevas went through all that trouble for a cover up for Horace Fletcher's funeral, well, what I discovered in my forensic work, confirms my belief. Now who are these two men, Tom Malone and Gerald Sheppard?"

"Well sir," began Jim Travis, "Tom Malone is the Supervisor or Superintendent of the Highway Commission and in charge of building the new highway through LaFouchfeye County. It will border on the government property belonging to Stennis Space Center. One of my sources, Jeannie Rose, swears that Gerald Sheppard is really Curtis Burras, who supposedly died in that Vancleave road fire, seven years ago."

"And," replied Dr. Tate, "I suppose Horace Fletcher handled the remains, correct?"

"That's right," smiled Bea.

"When I e-mailed and called my contacts in Washington, D.C., yesterday, I was told by more than one representative, that Congress was trying desperately to pass a bill concerning a lucrative land deal right smack in the middle of Mr. Malone's highway plans. In other words, somebody or lot's of somebody's stand to make a bundle of money. And I mean millions!"

"Okay," Bea said, "how did my Aunt Jewels, the dog Maggie May and Dr. Horatio Banks get tangled up in this web of deceit?"

"I can't say for sure Ms. Winslow, but I believe it was just bad timing on your Aunt's part."

"So," inquired Sheriff Travis, "you think Horace Fletcher is alive and master minded this scheme?"

"Could be, but no, not really. I think somebody else or…maybe his wife, Rose. Now that's what I wanted to meet you all for. Have you got anything?"

"Well Dr. Tate," began Jim, "Bea and I picked up the old car that her Aunt won in the drawing and Bea discovered dried blood specks on the front floor board."

Dr. Tate smiled. "I take it you sent them off for analysis."

"Yes sir….to my friend Mac Tavis. He said he's have it here by this evening. Dr. Tate, since we can't trust Mr. Luce, have you got anybody in mind that we can trust?"

"Sure do…my sister's boy, my nephew, Officer Barney Frye."

Bea began flipping her small note pad. After several pages, her fingers stopped. There was his name, Barney Frye, Bay St. Louis policeman. Bea smiled. "And he's your nephew? Great, that's great!"

CHAPTER 37

Pearl Talks to Deputy Paulie About Jeannie Rose and Bubba Cuevas

When he felt the light tap on his shoulder, Deputy Paulie turned quickly. "Oh, you startled me, Ms. Pearl!"

"I'm sorry, I thought that would be better than yelling out 'hey you'!"

"Have you got somethin' important on your mind, or can it wait thirty minutes?"

"I know, y'all stay so busy, now that Christmas is around the corner."

"Yes ma'am, how can I help you?"

"Deputy Paulie, I've been noticin' Jeannie Rose and Bubba Cuevas hangin' out together a lot these days."

"Is there somethin' wrong with that?"

"Well sir, in my day, girls didn't chase boys, you know what I mean?"

Deputy Paulie snickered a little, for he had heard more than one of the stories about Pearl's bloomin' errors. "Maybe he's a-courtin' her, you know, for the holidays. People always like to have somebody close for the holidays."

"Well Deputy Paulie, he's not just courtin', as you say, because he's seein' someone else too."

"You're not jealous, are you Ms. Pearl?"

"Who me? Why I wouldn't give Bubba Cuevas the time of day! Rose Fletcher might be interested however!"

"Well now, Ms. Pearl, Bubba works for Mrs. Fletcher and does moonlighting with Dr. Nathan Tate, in New Orleans."

"Did you know that Bubba Cuevas was at the Funeral Home that night, seven years ago when Mr. Fletcher was shot?"

"I don't recall that being mentioned in the trial."

"That's right, Deputy Paulie, because it wasn't!"

"Than how come you know about it?"

"Because, I was with him!"

Just then Deputy Taylor yelled, "Hey Paulie, that lady called for you again. You'd better get movin'!"

"Look, Ms. Pearl, I have to go right now, but can I talk to you later?"

"Sure you can. It's not like I have a shop to run anymore. I'll catch you later."

BEFORE AND AFTER

Main Street in Bay St. Louis, shown in April 2000, is lined with shops, restaurants and galleries.

Most of Main Street, except the area close to Beach Boulevard, was scarred but not destroyed by Hurricane Katrina.

Main Street in Bay St. Louis

Main Street reflects its name as the main artery in the heart of Bay St. Louis.

For years, it has offered a mix of locally owned art galleries, gift shops and restaurants, as well as professional businesses, many in converted houses that retained their porches and charm.

On the second Saturday of each month, merchants invited the public to nibble food, socialize and listen to music while they explored the Bay's quaint shops.

September's Second Saturday was canceled because it was too close to Katrina's visit, but on Oct. 8 it resumed — a little farther down Main Street.

The Front Beach shops are gone, as are some on the east end of Main, but Katrina did not zap the town spirit. Several hundred locals and people from other communities came to support the Bay that first post-Katrina Saturday.

"Main Street will come back. There is no doubt about it," said Mayor Eddie Favre. "Some business folks have already expressed returning, and now we're having Second Saturday every Saturday, not just once a month."

Each Saturday, Main Street bustles with more businesses, entrepreneurs selling things and more people to browse and buy.

"As we rebuild, we'll try to tie downtown into Main Street even better than before," said Favre. "Everyone was talking after the storm that we'll build back bigger and better. We don't necessarily need 'bigger' because our small-town atmosphere is what makes Bay St. Louis. But 'better' is good.

"The workers coming here to help us see what a unique community this is and they see the beauty here, despite what has happened. And it can only get better."

— KAT BERGERON

Richard and Dee Cichon. Picture taken in their Bay St.Louis, MS, home, September 2004.

Maggie May's Art & Gift Shop—June 11, 2005. Booksigning for 2nd book, Death Has No Appeal. A lovely couple who lived and worked in New Orleans, LA.

This was my "setup" for book signing at Maggie May's June 11, 2005.

Sylvia and Bill Stanton. Her artwork is displayed behind her.

The Bay St. Louis train tracks look like a twisted roller coaster ride. Beach Blvd. Bay St. Louis, MS.

Corner of Main St. and Beach Blvd. Looking down Main St. you can barely see Maggie May's green awning. A big pile of debris and sand are directly in front of it.

Lynn's mother in law, Chris Roberts, me and Lynn Roberts. Grand opening of Lynn's Business, The Calico House of Books Diamondhead, MS. August 2005—Destroyed two days later. (To be re-opened in May 2006).

The author standing in front of the remains of Maggie May's Gift, 2 weeks after Hurricane Katrina.

The back of Maggie May's where the individual artist's had showing of their work.

Some of the volunteers from Oklahoma who helped Bay St. Louis clean up.

My friend, Evelyn Hinton, stretching the awning of Maggie May's. Photo taken around September 19, 2005.

*One week later, September 26, 2005, the debris is removed. Progress
is slow but sure.*

*From the Bay St. Louis side of the demolished bridge. Just
cement pilings remain.*

*Looking left on Beach Blvd. All the pastel colored houses called "Chapel Hill"
were swept away.*

Observing the devastation of Hurricane Katrina to the beautiful Dock of the Bay Restaurant.

Dilapidated buildings ravaged by the monster storm, Katrina. Beach Blvd, Bay St. Louis, MS.

The businesses of Old Town on Front Beach in Bay St. Louis sat on a bluff overlooking the bay. *DOCK OF THE BAY—*

Front Beach, downtown Bay St. Louis

Front Beach was the charming door to downtown Bay St. Louis. With the bay side lined with small shops and restaurants, and more of the same on the west side of the beachfront road, it was a small-town mecca for arts, socializing, shopping and eating.

Katrina gouged out the road, the sandy bluffs and any buildings on the bay. The west side didn't fare much better, although shells of a few buildings still stand.

"It's important to save the charm of Bay St. Louis," said Mayor Eddie Favre.

"Prior to Katrina we had the best of all worlds but still had the small-town charm, and we're not willing to sacrifice that. Some have expressed concern that we would sell out to casinos and high-rise condominiums, but we're not for sale.

"Even though we lost some of the historical structure, we can restore some of that look by encouraging folks, as they develop and rebuild, to pick a pre-Camille, not pre-Katrina, façade on the beachfront and on Main Street.

"We may not be able to restore the buildings themselves, but we can have a similar appearance by tying into the Governor's Commission (on Recovery, Rebuilding and Renewal) and some of the tools we have available, like Smart-Codes, to guarantee mixed use and architectural design."

Such codes allow uniformity of rebuilding.

"There is hope," Favre said. "I can pretty much guarantee that we're not looking at anything like high-rise in the downtown area. We're not willing to give up what made Bay St. Louis a place apart."

Bay Town Inn, Bay St. Louis

Fulfilling a dream of owning a business that would use her knack of making people feel welcome and her love of gardening and cooking, Nikki Nicholson moved from New Orleans and bought Bay Town Inn Bed & Breakfast in 2003.

"When I saw the house, I knew if I didn't pursue it I'd have regrets. Katrina didn't make me sorry. I'm glad I did it," Nicholson said.

"Many of the guests who came will be friends for a lifetime. They came to the Bay not only to enjoy the inn and the shops and restaurants, but also the calming atmosphere that Bay St. Louis provided."

The art and antique-filled B&B at 208 North Beach Blvd. in the Bay was swept away. On the property stand two oaks, including the one that saved Nicholson, a dog and two others who made it to the tree when the 1899 house disintegrated.

Built by the deMonthzin family, the 4,600-square-foot house had eight guest rooms and a cottage and was turned into a B&B in 1991. The DeMonthzins used to tell the story of how that particular savior oak was a young tree about to be pulled up by a road crew when it was saved by the family.

"What's next?" said Nicholson. "As everybody is, I'm waiting on the outcome of insurance, possible SBA loans and for Beach Boulevard to be reconstructed because there is no more lawn in front of my house. I can't make any decisions until I know how I fare financially.

"My dream is to build another B&B in a style that would be right for the Bay St. Louis community."

— KAT BERGERON

PHOTOS BY JOHN FITZHUGH/SUN HERALD

In 1999, the DeMontluzin house that became Bay Town Inn Bed & Breakfast in Bay St. Louis turned 100 years old.

In back of this magnificent oak stood the Old Town Bed and Breakfast—Beach Blvd. Bay St. Louis, MS.

Bay St. Louis, Hancock Bank, Corner of Main St. and Beach Blvd. Asphalt, cement and dirt.

*Snapshot looking down Main Street from Hancock Bank.
More debris removed.*

*What is left of Ellen Kanes Gift Shop, on the service drive off of Highway 90.
One block from the Bay Bridge, Bay St. Louis, MS.*

The white picket fence surrounding the quaint yellow wooden famed house with the screened porch was washed away! Just propped up sign remains. Highway 90 service road, Bay St. Louis, MS.

Second Saturday was up and running! You can't keep Bay St. Louis down.
Oct. 8, 2005.

A high school classmate of mine from Galesburg, Patsy McGaghey and friend. They were helping Patsy's daughter Jill. She lived a block off the beach in Long Beach, MS and lost everything.

Balloons, fun, food and a band! Second Saturday was enjoyed by all! Bay St. Louis, MS. October 8, 2005.

Of course, "Survival" T-Shirts are a big sale item! October 8, 2005.

At Christmas time 2005, looking toward the water,
Main St., Bay St. Louis, MS.

As twilight settles…
Peace on earth…
Goodwill toward men.
Christmas 2005

Douglas Bristol and Dwight Isaacs, co-owners of The Shabby Chic, Main St., Bay St. Louis, MS. Famous for home-made chocolates and art boutique.

Another snapshot of The Shabby Chic, welcoming all to Second Saturday, May 13th, 2006.

Bay St. Louis, MS, Second Saturday, May 13ᵗʰ, 2006. The Artist Shop, Main St., a bustling place!

Bay St. Louis, MS, Second Saturday, May 13th, 2006. And the band played on and on and on....

A group of entrepreneurs, setting up shop for Second Saturday, May 13th, 2006. Bay St. Louis, MS.

Yummmmmmmm! Smells good! Hamburger and hotdogs cooking away. Come on folks, if you're hungry! Bay St. Louis, MS. Second Saturday, May 13th, 2006.

This team of sellers are settling in to display their wares. Bay St. Louis, MS, Second Saturday, May 13th, 2006.

CHAPTER 38

Jeannie Rose and Bubba Cuevas

"That was some party for Tommy Lockhart, wasn't it?" Bubba asked.

Jeannie Rose smiled, "Sure was. Ms Rose really knows how to throw a party. That's not why you asked me out for a boat ride, is it?"

"Nope. And it's not why I've started wantin' to see you either." With that remark, Bubba cut the engine and the boat began to glide slowly over the calm waters of the Bay.

"Jeannie Rose, I think…"

Jeannie Rose planted a kiss on his lips that sank him to his knees, which interrupted Bubba's thoughts and words. "Bubba Cuevas, I didn't come out here in this boat for you to make idle chatter, you hear? I know you like me, so why don't you show it?"

Up to now, Bubba had always been the aggressor, plowing over and ahead, but now, he wondered. Had he met his match? He had a hold of a wildcat, who was giving him a run for his money! Sure, he wanted some answers to a lot of questions and he had figured that Jeannie Rose could supply them, but even Bubba Cuevas wasn't ready for this!

Finally, he managed to untangle her legs from his waist and between the rapid kisses she was smothering him with, grab his breath! "Hold it! Sure Jeannie Rose, I like you, but really, I honestly wanted to talk…at least for a little while…then maybe…"

With that remark, Jeannie Rose leaned back, unwrapped her legs and sat on the backless cushion, and then proceeded to straighten her dress. "So, you probably think I do that a lot, huh? Well, I don't, and all that talk that those busybodies say about me, it's not true!"

Bubba heaved a deep sigh and cleared his throat. "I haven't heard anybody say anything, Jeannie Rose. But I know you could answer a few questions for me, say, about Curtis Burras?"

CHAPTER 39

Officer Barney Frye

Officer Barney Frye, Dr. Nathan Tate's nephew, had been a Bay St. Louis policeman for three years. As he sat at his desk and shuffled through his paperwork, his mind drifted back to a week ago, right before the kidnapping of Mrs. Julia McKenna and the dog, Maggie May. He just happened to be eating at Pirate's Cove, when they, two vacationers from Maine, fished the body out of the Gulf near Espy Avenue when his Uncle Nathan Tate arrived. After his external examination of the corpse, he and Barney reviewed their evidence over a cup of Java later at The Coffee Shop in Pass Christian.

"So," asked Uncle Nathan, "How's it been going for you, since your momma passed, Barney?"

"Not bad, sir. The guys down at the station and some of their wives have really helped me out. Everything going fine over your way?"

"Never better! Crime is still a major factor. But I would be out of job if it weren't, now wouldn't I?"

They both laughed. "Say Barney, I hear that Dr. Horatio Banks is going to give a speech at The Dock of the Bay. You going?"

"No, I can't actually hear it. I'll be on duty."

"That's too bad. A friend of mine, Bea Winslow, heard him speak at a convention in Jackson. Said he was good, real good."

"I've heard of her. She solved that murder about a Judge a year or two ago. Got her Aunt out of jail, I believe."

CHAPTER 40

Bea Gets A Surprise Visit From Mac Tavis And Results About Specks of Dried Blood

When the doorbell rang, Bea rolled over and tried to focus on her alarm clock. Who could that be at 6:00 a.m.? After the second chime, came a loud, forceful knock. "All right! All right...I'm coming!" she screamed. "You don't have to knock the door down! Mac! What on earth are you doing here?"

"You know Bea, I asked myself that same question, the last time I arrived."

"Well...what ARE you doing here?"

"I brought the results of your REQUEST....and after I dug into the past copies of The Sea Coast Echo, Sun Herald and The Bay Press...1 figured you might need old Mac's services....again."

"Come on in and I'll make us some coffee."

"Where's your Aunt?"

Bea stopped and looked at him. "You mean you haven't heard?"

"Heard what Bea?"

"Aunt Jewels was kidnapped, four days ago."

"You're kidding!"

"No, I'm serious. She and Captain Eric were shopping in a little gift shop called Maggie May's, in the Bay. They had gone there to hear Dr. Horatio Banks give a speech at The Dock of the Bay on the environment and to pick up her *Cruisin' The Coast* prize. She had won a 1927 Model T. Ford."

"So...what happened?"

"Well, it seems, someone had kidnapped Dr. Banks and they also stopped in Maggie May's Gift Shop. Aunt Jewels probably recognized the Doctor and the kidnappers took her and the dog."

"What about the Captain? Wait a minute. Did you say, a dog?"

"Yes, Maggie May's Gift Shop is named after a dog and Aunt Jewels thought she had lost an earring and told Eric she was going back into the shop. She thought she lost it while she was petting the dog. Well she never came back out!"

"Oh! Now I understand why all the questions about Barry Luce!" Mac exclaimed.

"Yes...supposedly he's in charge of the case...about Dr. Banks, but he also questioned the proprietors of Maggie May's and their assistant, about my Aunt's disappearance."

Mac squinted over his Ben Franklin eyeglasses and replied, "and the dog, right? I hope you don't believe those dried blood specks belong to your Aunt, because they don't."

"Whew! That's a relief! But Mac, can you identify them?"

"Sure can, and did! Remember, I told you I've done some digging. Well Bea, I uncovered some interesting news and facts. Dr. Banks has a rare genetic blood type and some of those specks were his....but it gets more interesting. The majority of those little specks of dried blood belong to...."

At that very moment, Bea's cell phone jangled, '*When The Saints Come Marchin' In*'. "Hello?"

"Hey, it's me, Jim."

"I know who it is!"

"I must have woke you up....and I truly apologize."

"No Jim, I'm awake. Mac woke me up about twenty minutes ago. What's your excuse?"

"I have a bit of news and wanted to share it with my favorite girl."

Now......Bea pondered about that. She really couldn't stay angry. "Oh? Really now."

Mac stood up and started strolling toward the door.

"Wait a minute Jim." Covering the phone, Bea stepped forward and stopped him. "Oh, no you don't. Mac, you have to finish what you were telling me....you know, about the blood. Whose was it?" Holding Mac back with her hand placed firmly against his chest, she continued talking to Jim. "You still there? Good! Come on out! Bye now. Mac, you sit back down. Now......tell me...before anything else happens. Whose blood is it?"

CHAPTER 41

At The Hideout
6:00 a.m., December 22ⁿᵈ

"Rise and shine, it's breakfast time!" Mousy proclaimed while flicking on the one lone exposed light bulb.

Horatio Banks, Jr., rolled over and looked to his right. "Dad? What in God's name are you doing here?"

Aunt Jewels propped herself up on one elbow and replied, "And who are you?"

"Mrs. McKenna, this is my son, Horatio Banks, Jr. Son, let me introduce you to Mrs. Julia McKenna and the dog's name is Maggie May. Say, by any chance, did you receive my message?"

"About what?"

Dr. Banks quickly glanced around to make sure no one was listening, but didn't see the wrapped up bundle in the far corner of the room. "Do you remember when I said 'Dog gone Christmas'?"

"Yes dad," he chuckled, "I remember that crazy message. Is that why that dog is here?"

"No it isn't, but she's a part of it now."

Aunt Jewels rolled her eyes upward, looked back at the doctor and asked, "How so?"

"Because," Dr. Banks continued to whisper, "I slipped that digital operational gadget for the manual launch into that dog's blankets."

Like a phoenix rising from the ashes, came an elderly whiskered man from underneath the mountain of rags, and proclaimed, "I'm tellin' Mousy!"

Aunt Jewels sat straight up. "Amos Seals! What in tarnation are you doing in here?"

"I don't rightly know Ms. Julia, but after your niece and that Sheriff got your prize, you know the Model T., some lady came by and asked me for directions. While I was pointin' one way, she chloroformed me and I just now woke up hearing this here doc saying about somethin' in that dog's blanket and I figure that might be my ticket out of here!"

"And just how do you figure that?" Ms. Julia smarted back.

"Because," he stuttered, "I wasn't completely under when they threw me in the back set, and I heard her yappin' over her cell phone about a important little gadget!"

"You said 'they', Amos," she quizzed.

"Yeah…"

"Well….? Was it a man and a woman, or two women, or what?"

Amos started rubbing his whiskers. "Well, I reckin' it was a man and that woman."

Just then Mousy unlocked the door again and kicked it wide open. "Here's your breakfast folks. Some eggs, grits, coffee and a slab of ham!"

CHAPTER 42

It's Three Days Till Christmas Sheriff Travis Arrives At Bea's House

"Like I was saying Mac, whose blood is it?" asked Bea.

"Looks like we got company," smiled Mac.

"I know, I know Mac, will you please answer my question?"

As Sheriff Travis came in the door, he extended his hand to Mac, "Bea said you were here. Glad to see you."

"All right," begged Bea, "enough formalities, you two. Mac, please give me the results."

"The majority of the dried specks of blood belonged to Horace Fletcher," smiled Mac.

"But he was killed seven years ago. Shot in the chest at Shady Rest Funeral Home!"

"Bea," Mac continued, "I'm thinking that maybe this Fletcher guy was murdered somewhere else and transported to the funeral home and put in his office."

"Or," Sheriff Travis added, "it could be a possibility that he's not dead at all. If you remember Bea, Rose Fletcher had a closed casket at his funeral because supposedly she couldn't bear to look at him lying there."

"Okay," Bea replied, tapping her fingers on the kitchen table. "He must have been transported there in that old car, but by whom?"

"Did you get a bill of sale?" asked Mac.

"No…., Amos Seals is giving the papers to me later. Jim and I just wanted to pick up Aunt Jewels' prize."

"Well Bea," Mac began, "whoever that car is registered to, might have an inkling to what is going on, you know."

Just then, Sheriff Travis' cell phone jangled *'Anchor's Aweigh'*. "Hello? Yes…when did you discover this? I see. I understand. I agree, maybe it's nothing, but, yes, I realize he was a steady worker. No, that's perfectly all right. Yes, I will certainly look into it. Thanks and goodbye."

Both Bea and Mac looked at Jim, then asked, "who was that?"

"Ann Peterson of The Bay Town Bed and Breakfast. It seems Amos Seals didn't show up for work."

Again, the Sheriffs phone rang. "Hello? Yes, Officer Frye. I just got a call, mentioning that very same thing. Are you there now? Oh, I see….and what did Ann Peterson tell you? Thanks Officer Frye. Bye. Well folks that was Officer Frye. He and Officer Trace went over to talk to Amos Seals and like Ann Peterson told me, Amos didn't show up for work. However, she told Officer Frye that last night, one of her boarders saw Amos talking to a heavy set woman with jet black hair. The boarders' bedroom window faces the alley and she overheard the lady ask Mr. Seals for directions. The next minute he was gone."

"That's not good," replied Bea. "Okay Jim, what's your other news?"

"Officer Barney Frye, Dr. Tate's nephew stopped by the office with some interesting information. The cast he made of the tire prints behind Maggie May's are of a 1927 Model T. Ford. That could be the car your Aunt won, and was used to transport Dr. Banks, your Aunt and the dog to where ever they are being held."

Bea hit the table with her fist. "And of course, we don't know where! Now, Amos Seals has disappeared."

"Bea," Mac began, "I think our best bet is to try to gain confidence with Barry Luce. I have a suggestion. Mr. Luce doesn't know me, so I will work on him. Sheriff, you are more familiar with Tom Malone and Bea, how much do you really know about Rose Fletcher?"

"Okay," Bea agreed, "I think your idea is great. Don't you think so Jim?"

With a nod of Jim's head, Bea smiled.

Mac rubbed his hands together, "Now mates, also in my readings, I discovered the powers that be in Washington, D.C., want a land bill to pass that includes one hundred thousand acres that surround Stennis Space Center, past the buffer zone. Of course you realize that's the land that Tom Malone has been purchasing."

"Mac," grinned Bea, "the beauty shop and the funeral home are directly adjacent to it."

Mac laughed out loud. "Don't I know it! Listen, one of the men keeping a rather low profile is a fella by the name of Gerald Sheppard. He's a good friend of Tom Malone. Now the way I figure it, we haven't got much time. Congress wants that bill to pass, so all of them can be home for Christmas."

"Mac," replied Jim, "One of my sources swears that Curtis Burras is using the name of Gerald Sheppard."

Mac looked up with questioning eyes. "And you can believe your source?"

Both Bea and Jim nodded yes.

"It's three days till Christmas," replied Bea.

"I know my dear," Mac answered. "That's why we have to uncover their scheme and find out where Aunt Jewels, Dr. Banks and the dog are!" "Let's do it!" Exclaimed Jim.

CHAPTER 43

Jeannie Rose Tells Bubba About Curtis Burras

"What is it you want to know about Curtis?" quizzed Jeannie Rose.

"Well, I hear tell you knew him way back, say, seven years ago," replied Bubba.

"And what if I did? What is it to you? You gonna send him a birthday card maybe?"

"Look Jeannie Rose, I'm gonna be comin' into some big money, I mean really big money and I want to know who all the competition is. You understand that, don't ya?"

"Well, I want to find him for another reason."

"Oh yeah? What?"

"He killed my brother Bennie and burnt down the house, with him in it. Then he carried me out to the front yard and tried to kill me, but I guess his aim was off, because he just grazed my forehead. He thought I was dead."

"So, how did you happen to come into all that money?"

"Bubba, an old couple found me and took me in and adopted me. They were financially well off. When they passed, I began my search for him."

"And it brought you back to Lafouchfeye County?"

"Sure enough. He's a big land developer now and does business with some of the men who help run this country."

"Do you know where he's at?"

Tossing her hair back over her shoulders, she smirked. "Would I be here with you, if I knew where I could find him? And besides, you admitted it Bubba, that's really why you brought me out here on Ghost Bayou Lake."

It was Bubba's turn to get passionate and he grabbed Jeannie Rose, pressing his lips on hers. "Now you can believe what you want, but Jeannie Rose, how would you like to go fishin' with me down in Jamaica?"

CHAPTER 44

Mac Tavis Visits Barry Luce At Stennis Space Center At Noon, 22 December 2005

Mac couldn't help but notice the manicured grounds outside the office of Chief Detective Barry Luce. After stepping inside to the foyer, a petite brunette secretary, wearing a dazzling smile, instantly greeted him. "Yes," she sighed, batting her long eyelashes, "May I help you?"

"My name is Mac Tavis and I have a 12:00 o'clock appointment with Detective Luce."

"Yes sir, he's expecting you. His office is down the hall, first door to your right."

"Thank you." Mac hadn't taken three steps when Barry Luce met him in the hallway. "I appreciate you seeing me on such short notice, Mr. Luce."

"Please, call me Barry, it's less formal and we don't have to be formal, do we? Have a seat, over there, by the credenza."

"I'll get right to the point Mr....sorry, Barry," Mac began. "Several incidents have taken place, that I'm not sure if you're aware of."

"Such as?"

"For one thing, Horatio Banks, Jr. is alive and not dead, and Bea Winslow and I are not sure that Horace Fletcher died seven years ago."

"Now, that's a stretch, Mac," smiled Barry.

"It seems so, but let me run this by you. There's a land bill on hold in Washington, D.C., right now, that has to be passed and signed before Christmas. Tom Malone has already bought Pearl's Beauty Shop and is supposed to purchase the Shady Rest Funeral Home."

"Listen, Tom Malone has been buying the land adjacent to Stennis Space Center for a connecting road. That's been in the works for a number of years and that doesn't affect me. No, I'm concerned with the disappearance of Dr. Horatio Banks."

"I believe it's all connected Barry. Here's another piece of information. Bea's Aunt, Mrs. Julia McKenna, Dr. Banks and the dog, Maggie May were transported to an undisclosed place in a 1927 Model T. Ford that Mrs. McKenna had won in a drawing, two months previously."

"And you determined this by.....how? Are you positive it's the same car? In October we held 'Cruisin' The Coast' and I can't begin to tell you the number of 1927 Model T. Ford's we had registered."

"A plaster cast of the tire tracks were made outside the back door of the Gift Shop."

Suddenly the phone rang. Barry Luce held up his index finger. "Just a minute, Mac. Hello? I told you, Miss Penny, hold all my calls....that's correct...all of them. Sorry Mac, you were saying?"

Mac's training indicated Barry Luce's mannerisms and attitude were showing all the signs of frustration. "Look Barry," continued Mac, just one more question. Have you ever heard of a Mr. Gerald Sheppard?"

"Sheppard? No, the name doesn't ring a bell. Is he with the FBI or local law enforcement?"

"No, not that I know of. Anyway, thanks for your time."

"No problem at all. Glad to do it. I certainly hope your friend, Bea Winslow finds her Aunt soon."

"Don't bother showing me to the door. You have work to do. See you later." As luck would have it, the secretary, Miss Penny, was quietly buffing her long nails while sitting at her desk. Mac was willing to take big chance. He quickly turned on his Scottish charm. "Ma'am, I'm terribly sorry that I got you in trouble, when you transferred that call to Detective Luce."

She smiled sweetly. "Sometimes here lately, he's been on edge. I remember earlier, he said he was expecting an important call."

"From who?" Mac inquired.

"Well, Mr. Tavis, I'm really not supposed to discuss business with clients."

Mac leaned over the desk and gazed into her eyes. "We're good friends, you can tell me."

"Well...., Gerald can be really persistent sometimes."

"Gerald Sheppard?"

"Why yes, do you know him?"

"Not personally Miss Penny. Look, thanks a lot and let's keep in touch, okay? Oh, Mr. Luce mentioned a big gathering that takes place in October. I believe he called it *'Cruisin The Coast'*. Do you happen to know who's in charge of it?"

Miss Penny grinned from ear to ear. "Why, that's an easy one. Mr. Luce was and still is!"

"Thanks my wee lassy! Gotta go now!"

Mac was no sooner out the door and down the staircase, when Barry Luce turned the corner and entered the waiting room. "I thought I heard voices, Miss Penny."

"You did sir. I was talking to......my mother on the phone."

At The Hideout

"You made a very wise decision Amos," winked Aunt Jewels.

"Well the fact that I'm still here and locked up, doesn't set very well with me!"

"Look Amos," Aunt Jewels continued, "It doesn't set well with any of us. We're not exactly sure what the devil is going on. Dr. Banks was just going to give a talk on the environment and somebody has substituted a dead body for his son. How did we get to this place anyway?"

Amos paused, took a sip of black coffee and then said, "Ms. Julia, those two hoodlums outside called Mousy and Meathead, was with an old gal I've never seen before. They came to the Bed & Breakfast and asked me if they could borrow the old car. They said it was some kind of antique car show just around the corner, in back of the bank. I hadn't heard of any, but things happen quickly, sometimes in setting up a place, so I said okay, you can borrow it."

"Are you telling me they brought us out here in the car that I won in the lottery?"

"That's right. The Doc here plus you and the dog."

"Dr. Banks," remarked Aunt Jewels, "the reason I went back in the Gift Shop was because I thought I'd lost one of Bea's earrings, that I had borrowed. I found a small metal cylinder-type gizmo in Maggie May's blankets, while I was rummaging around."

Dr. Banks became very quiet. "Ma'am, where is the computer chip?"

"What? Oh, I have it in my bos....I have it hidden. Why?"

"Ma'am, I believe that is what those men are after."

"Why? What is it dad?" Banks, Jr. asked.

"It has to be manually inserted into the mechanism, for the space shuttle to operate properly, son. If it were to get into the wrong hands…well, it just can't that's all."

Aunt Jewels looked down the front of her dress. "You mean this little gizmo can launch a space rocket? Gee! I feel like Helen of Troy and that Trojan Horse!"

"Mrs. McKenna….," began the Doctor.

"Oh please, call me Julia or Aunt Jewels."

"All right then, Aunt Jewels, we cannot let them have that 'gizmo', as you call it, under any circumstances!"

"They wouldn't dare touch it, not where I have it!" declared Aunt Jewels.

"Also, we mustn't let them know we are on to their little scheme," whispered the Doctor, through pursed lips. "Son, do you have any idea why they faked your death?"

"I believe it had to do with me getting Cyrus Dedeaux out of Parchman. I can't think of anything else. Look, I'm still trying to figure out your crazy message."

Dr. Banks chuckled under his breath. "Son, I said dog gone Christmas."

"So?"

"Dog stands for 'digital operational gadget'."

"And," Banks Jr. asked, "What does Christmas stand for?"

His father smiled. The twenty-fifth is Christmas and the launch is in twenty-five days."

Amos looked at the three of them and said, "Well, I'll be horn swaggled." He quickly turned his attention to Aunt Jewels.

Her eyes flashing, Aunt Jewels spit out her words. "Amos Seals! If you so much as open your mouth, I'll knock you from here to kingdom come, you hear me?"

CHAPTER 46

Sheriff Travis Talks With Tom Malone

As Sheriff Jim Travis pulled up to the excavation site, he saw Tom Malone talking on his cell phone. "Hi there Tom!"

Tom glanced over his shoulder. "Yeah, he's here. I'll talk to you later. Good afternoon Sheriff. I understand by my answering service you wanted to see me."

"That's right. A lot of things are happening might fast and to tell you the truth, I wanted to be sure all of us were on the same page."

While Tom folded up his cell phone and shoved it in his jacket pocket, he nodded his head in agreement. "I know just how you feel Sheriff. So many things have been taking place, sometimes you don't know which end is up."

"Oh, I don't know about that Tom. I try to keep my ends covered. Do you know a Gerald Sheppard?"

He had caught Tom off guard. "Who?"

"Gerald Sheppard. I've heard he's a land developer and a friend of yours."

"I know of him, but he and I don't travel in the same circles."

"So what you're saying is he's in with the big boys in Washington, D.C.?"

"I don't follow you Sheriff."

"Well then, let me clear the cobwebs away and show you a clean path. I think you and Gerald Sheppard are in cahoots about a land buying scheme that will net you both millions of dollars."

The jangle of *'Semper Fidilis'* on Tom's cell phone, broke up the conversation. "Excuse me.....Yes......I see, that could be probable at this time. No, I'll get back with you later. Sheriff Travis, I'm a busy man at the moment. If you would like to resume this conversation later on at your office, that would be fine, but I really must get back to work."

"Think about what I said Mr. Malone."

"Oh I will Sheriff, I most definitely will!" Tom's phone rang again. "Hey, yeah...he's gone, just left. No way, we can't do that. Do you realize you're talking about mass murder? No...there's got to be a better way. Wait a minute. Bea Winslow just got out of her car and is walking up the front porch steps to The Shady Rest Funeral Home."

CHAPTER 47

Maudelle Overhears Charlie's Phone Call

She absolutely hated shopping. It didn't matter whether it was for groceries or presents; Maudelle detested the idea of waiting in line for anything. After arriving home, she began hauling in the bags of food. That was another thing. Nobody was there to help her! Pearl was always gone. Maudelle didn't realize her sister had such an active social life. Her nephew Timmy had run off to New Orleans with two friends he had met at The Tiny Diner. No, Maudelle had no one to help her unload her car, help with the laundry and take care of Charlie! Speaking of Charlie, where was he? Usually he was sitting out on the front porch, over by the swing. She just realized he wasn't around. "Charlie?" she yelled. No answer. After putting the frozen articles away, she slowly walked through to the dining room. Again she muttered, "Charlie?" Where was he?

Approaching his bedroom, she heard the T. V. advertising a trampoline for $600.00, complete with safety railings. Opening the door, she glanced around the entire room. Maybe he was in the bathroom. She knocked softly and whispered, "Charlie?" Charlie was not to be found. Maudelle was completely confused. The man was in a wheelchair. He had to be nearby, but where?

After searching through the entire first floor, she again headed toward the kitchen patio. There, parked by the back screen door, was Charlie's wheelchair, minus Charlie! Immediately, Maudelle's eyes started scanning every inch of their backyard. As her eyes settled on the backside of their decaying faded red barn, she saw Charlie's silhouette against the broad beam of the door! How could this be? Seven years ago, his spine had been severed, Dr. Wills had said he'd never walk again, but there he was, smoking a cigarette and standing upright, talking on that damn little cell phone. The one that Maudelle had bought him, just in case he had an emergency he could call her at work!

Quickly she ran back to the front of the house, out the door and around the neighbors' yard. Now carefully climbing through the barbwire fence, she snuck up directly opposite of where Charlie was standing. He was laughing and saying, "no, I understand perfectly. No she doesn't know a thing. Look honey, we have waited seven years for this, a few days longer are not gonna make a big difference. I love you too; you know that and have for a good time now. I told you, we have to be careful. She went to make groceries. Hey, now baby, I really have to go and get back in my wheelchair. Yeah, baby, I love you. Bye."

CHAPTER 48

Bea Winslow and Rose Fletcher Meet At The Shady Rest Funeral Home The Time is 1:00 p.m., 22 December 2005

The Shady Rest Funeral Home had the prettiest pristine stucco porch on the block. White wicker furniture decorated the front area with lush green palm fern swaying in the breeze. You could almost imagine a social gathering of the elite, after a wake, sipping mint juleps and sharing the latest gossip. Bea's hand was just about to turn the brass chime, when Rose Fletcher opened the beveled glass door and greeted her with a large hug and a kiss. "You don't know how happy I was that you called and wanted to see me!"

Although stunned, Bea replied, "I'm glad also."

"Would you like to sit out here, on the veranda or take tea in the parlor?"

"Mrs. Fletcher, the veranda would be just fine."

"Good. I'll have Maudelle bring us some tea and beignets. You will simply love them. She makes them from scratch, of course."

"What did you call them?"

"Beignets. They are a French doughnut. Delicious, simply delicious!"

"I've had them at Cafe de Monde in New Orleans. Maudelle's been with you for a time now, hasn't she?"

"Oh mercy, yes. Seven years. Soon to be eight. I'll be back in a minute." Rose disappeared around the corner and down the hall. She hurriedly dialed Maudelle's number. Tapping her right foot, she moaned, "Answer, you dim wit."

"Hello?" Maudelle spoke abruptly. "Oh, yes ma'am. Now? I suppose so," she drawled. "Sure, I'll be there shortly."

A slight breeze caught Rose's purple and pink ruffled chiffon dress as she twittered back through the hallway and out the front door. "Mercy! I'd better be careful Ms. Winslow. All the neighbors will be talkin'! Now why did I say that? We do not have anymore neighbors!"

"Mrs. Fletcher......"

"Please......, call me Rose. Everyone else does. Tell me, have you heard anything about your Aunt?"

"No ma'am, nothing yet."

Straightening her skirt, Rose replied, "I understand a Mr. Luce is in charge of the investigation."

"Do you know Mr. Luce, Rose?"

"Mercy yes. Horace and I have been acquainted with Mr. Luce for years. Why I remember...but wait, you don't want to hear me reminisce."

"Rose, do you know why Tom Malone wants to buy your property?"

"Why yes, silly. Some old highway is supposed to go through here, but you know what? I don't think I'm selling."

"Oh, why?"

"This has been our business and part time home for so long, and well, I'd prefer to stay right here. Besides, his old highway can just detour around our four acres of land."

Bea stirred her tea, and then smiled. "I guess people think that since Horace is gone, you'd might be better off selling and living in another part of the county."

The look of surprise overtook Rose's face, but quickly faded as Maudelle sashayed through the doorway, approaching the two ladies, with more tea and beignets. "You know Maudelle Perkins, don't you, Bea?" smiled Rose.

"Why yes ma'am, I do. It's good to see you again. How's your sister Pearl doing, since she has gained a few more dollars?" Bea inquired.

"Pearl is fine, Ms. Bea. Never better. Will that be all, Ms. Rose?"

"Yes Maudelle, and thank you."

After Bea nibbled on another beignet, she appropriately dabbed her mouth with the pale green linen napkin Ms. Rose had provided. "Ms. Rose," began Bea, "Were you here that night when your husband Horace was shot?"

As Rose sipped her tea, she paused. "Excuse me dear?"

"I said, were you around that evening, seven years ago?"

"Mercy me, no I wasn't."

"All right then, do you own a 1927 Model T. Ford?"

"My goodness Bea! You are inquisitive, aren't you? As a matter of fact, Horace and I did have an old Ford, but he sold it."

"Really? Who to?"

"Our good friend, Detective Barry Luce."

"And when was this Ms. Rose?"

"Oh honey, that's been years ago."

"You don't say? Something like....seven years ago?"

Rose quietly replaced her teacup upon the silver tray. "Ummm," she demurely replied, "something like that. Excuse me Bea, but why did you ask if I were here when Horace was shot?"

"I just thought, maybe, you had driven him over."

Rose began tapping her finger on her forehead. "Now, I was thinking that, because, after all, you are a private investigator and you have to ask all kinds of questions. Well dear, as a matter of fact, I did drive him here and briefly spoke with Bubba Cuevas, one of our morticians. But then I left. Horace was suppose to call me later, you know, to come pick him up. Of course, this was all brought out in the inquest, you realize."

Bea nodded in agreement. "Yes, yes, of course it was."

Rose retrieved her handkerchief from her bosom and began dabbing her right eye. "I was visitin' a sick Aunt......in the next county."

"Oh, yes ma'am, I understand. Would that be Moriah County, Ms. Rose?"

"No honey, Harrison County."

CHAPTER 49

Dr. Nathan Tate Meets With Sheriff Travis And Introduces Dr. Marcus Donald, FBI

Before leaving his office, Sheriff Travis phoned Bea and told her where he was going. Except for the fact she was still with Mrs. Fletcher, he would loved to have her along for the drive over to New Orleans. He smiled to himself as he thought of his surprise Christmas present to her last Christmas. Those turquoise earrings looked stunning on her. What he really wanted to give her was a ring, but he knew that was out of the question.

The ride over to Dr. Tate's office was quicker than he thought. In no time at all, he was parking his car on the third floor of the garage adjacent to Nathan's office. Getting out of his Jeep, he couldn't help but notice Nathan's SUV parked in the next slot, but whose Mercedes was next to his?

Since Dr. Tate's secretary had already left for the day, he'd informed the security guard of Sheriff Travis' arrival.

"Hi there Cecil," smiled the Sheriff.

"Must be somethin' mighty important, to call you over."

"Say, Cecil, whose car is that parked next to the doc's?"

Cecil looked over his shoulder, and then stepped closer. "Some big wig from Washington, D.C. His ID. reads Dr. Marcus Donald. He's been up there for about two hours now."

Sheriff Travis chuckled. "Well, best I mosey on up there. Don't want to keep the two Doctors waiting."

"See you later, son."

As the Sheriff stepped off the elevator, he heard both men chattering away. In fact he hated to interrupt their conversation. "Well, Nathan, I finally got here."

"Good......, Jim. Let me introduce you to an old friend and colleague of mine, Dr. Marcus Donald. He works with the FBI in Washington, D.C., but out of the Virginia office. He's been telling me some interesting tales about our friend, Detective Barry Luce."

"So you're the infamous Sheriff of LaFouchfeye County, that Nathan admires so much. I'm really glad to make your acquaintance."

Jim couldn't help but give him the once over. He judged him to be about six feet, sandy colored hair, with a hint of grey and dark piercing eyes.

"Have a seat," continued Dr. Donald, "and let me catch you up on all our findings. I understand you also work with a Private Investigator named Bea Winslow?"

"Yes sir, I do, and I might add she's a darned good one too!"

Marcus smiled. "You don't have to sell me Sheriff; I worked with her and Mac Tavis a number of years ago. Now, first off, we know that Barry Luce orchestrated the entire kidnapping of Dr. Horatio Banks as a cover up for the covert plan involving the land scheme. I've checked into Tom Malone's background and discovered he is up to his ears in money laundering and fraud."

Dr. Tate added, "I've informed Marcus of the kidnapping of Bea's Aunt and the dog, Maggie May. We both agree, it was the timing and circumstance which involved them, but with the severity of national security, their lives could be in danger."

"So, what do we do?" asked Sheriff Travis.

"Well sir, we're going to flush them out!" smiled Dr. Donald. You're going to do it from your end and I'm headed back to D.C. and talk with the committee chairman handling that land acquisition."

CHAPTER 50

Tom Malone and Gerald Sheppard At Buccaneer Park 7:00 p.m., 22 December

Since it was almost deserted during the winter season, Tom Malone figured Buccaneer Park would be the ideal place to meet Gerald Sheppard. Time was running out. Tom had been contacted by Luce, and told to finish the deal, or he was going to end up like the people they had tied up in the old hideout cabin. Why wasn't his charm working on Rose Fletcher? He had certainly spent enough time with her. She was putting off signing over the property, but why? There had to be a reason. He had checked and rechecked all the property taxes, location, mineral rights......wait a minute. He hadn't checked on that one. Bubba Cuevas told him it was okay. Maybe there was something underneath those four acres of land that even he didn't know about. Just then, a White Diamond taxicab pulled up.

"Thanks Mac," replied Gerald Sheppard, as he jumped out of the cab and started rushing towards the small gazebo, where Tom Malone was waiting. "Looks like we're in for a little squall," Gerald smirked.

Tom was agitated. "Look, I didn't come out here to talk about the weather, Sheppard. What's on your mind?"

"The powers that be in Washington, D.C. say you have to move and move fast! That bill has to pass tomorrow, December 23rd, by four o'clock in the afternoon! I hope you have convinced that broad to sell!"

"Honest to God, Sheppard, I have done everything I can think of to convince her to sign the property over to me. Now she's thinking that maybe…"

"There's no maybe, Malone! Luce told me you were hedging on this deal. I told him he was crazy. Now we need that property and we need her to sign it over now! Aren't you supposed to see her tonight, later on?"

"Yeah…later on."

"Well…do what you have to do. Put your whole heart into it! I'm telling you Malone, these guys play for keeps! Oh yeah, by the way, you going home for Christmas?"

Tom gave him a side-glance. "Yeah, I'll probably make it home by then. Crissy's working on a huge tax case; however, she's planning a quiet dinner for us." Just then Tom's cell phone rang. "It's Crissy. Hi hon.…oh, just hanging around. What? Well, I'll miss you to, but I totally understand how work can mess things up. How long will you be tied up? No, really, I understand sweetheart. Don't worry, I'll manage. Love you."

"So, Malone," smiled Sheppard, you have a change of plans?"

"Yeah, Crissy said she was going to be bogged down for a week!"

"That's too bad Malone. Well, you know what you have to do, so do it…and fast! Now, do you mind dropping me off at The Tiny Diner? I haven't eaten yet."

CHAPTER 51

Bea Tells Sheriff Travis Of Her Plan

"Well? Did you have any luck, Jim?" Bea asked.

"Sure, at least I believe so. Malone's a slippery cuss, but personally, I think he's in over his head. What did you come up with, about Rose?"

"I think Horace is alive!"

"I do too!" Jim smiled, "I've believed it ever since Mac got those blood samples back!"

"But, proving it is something else. I also checked the records at the county courthouse, you know about Tom Malone acquiring the land, for the supposed highway. Oh sure, there's a plan, but it doesn't include Pearl's Beauty Shop and The Shady Rest Funeral Home. No, there's something else on his agenda about those two properties. I have a plan, Jim. I admit it's risky, but we are running out of time."

"Okay, tell me about it."

"I want you to travel to Washington, D.C. and stop the land proceedings!"

"Me? Why me?"

"Because.... it's in your jurisdiction, that's why!"

"Okay......you must have a good reason......mind telling me what it is?"

"Look Jim, Mac told me that Dr. Marcus Donald met with you and Dr. Tate..."

"You know about that?"

Bea smiled. "Jim, there's not much I don't know about," and gave him a quick peck on his lips. "I want you to travel back with Dr. Donald……and……I have another small plan in mind. I'm going to make sure Bubba Cuevas gets a free phone card."

"And?"

"To check who he calls."

"So how are you going to do that?"

"I'm going to disguise myself as a promotional marketing advertiser and tell him he's won a phone card worth…., say, 200 minutes. What I hope he'll do is call his partners in crime, so we can find out where they have Aunt Jewels and the dog hidden."

"Where did you come up with that idea, Bea?"

"Well, I admit it's not an original thought, but I saw it mentioned in The Sun Herald, so I figured, why not? It worked for them and Bubba isn't a rocket scientist!"

"You got that right. Well, if I'm going to D.C. and with Dr. Donald, I'd better get moving!"

As Bea started for the door, Jim cleared his throat. "Aren't you forgetting something?"

Bea stopped and turned around. "Oh yeah…." And quickly moved closer to him. "You mean this?" After their long embrace, Bea gazed deeply into Jim's eyes. "You be careful in the capital. You realize there are twelve women to every man up there."

"I'm not interested."

"Oops!" Apologized Deputy Paulie. "Sorry to interrupt!"

"I was just leaving," Bea grinned.

CHAPTER 52

The Shady Rest Funeral Home

This time, Tom Malone left his car at the motel and took a taxi. After letting himself in with his key, he proceeded down the hallway of the funeral home, to the parlor with the mirror ceiling. He had called her and prearranged their meeting. She sat alone, in the shadows. The crimson glow of the tip of her cigarette illuminated the back of the room.

"We have to talk," he said, quietly.

"Not right at this moment," she replied.

"Decisions have to be made, tonight," he urged.

"And they will be, but not now. Look, we don't have much time," and quickly crushed out her cigarette in a small disposable tin.

"Don't I know it," he muttered, before she began smothering his face with kisses.

CHAPTER 53

Dr. Tate Informs Sheriff Travis About The Bones Discovered At The Beauty Shop Excavation

Even Dr. Nathan Tate was surprised when he received the results. Of course he would let Tom Malone know, but first he'd notify Sheriff Travis and Ms. Winslow. After getting the documents, he did some more research on his own. There had been an extensive write up in The Clarion Ledger about Joseph Fletcher, the rebellious youth of Mr. and Mrs. Horace Fletcher, and some twenty years ago. He had been caught red handed in a burglary sting and had been sentenced to seven years at Parchman penitentiary. His father made the statement that, "Joseph was no longer a son of his!"

Just then, Dr. Tate's phone rang. "Hello? Good...good, I'm glad you received my message. No, I didn't want to leave the news with anybody but you. Hold your horses, Jim. I have the results of the bones found in the beauty shop. They belong to Joseph Fletcher, the long lost son of Rose and Horace Fletcher. I know, I know, it was a surprise to me too. Look, I was hoping you and I and Ms. Winslow could get together. Yes, I know it's late. Oh, I see. Well if you can't, ask Ms. Winslow if she can meet with me. Really? Okay, put her on. Hi, Ms. Winslow, I knew you'd be happy about that discovery. I agree, but of course I have to let Mr. Malone know. He'll want to continue his digging. Why do you believe that Horace Fletcher is still alive? Oh......I see. Well, be careful driving over."

CHAPTER 54

Tom Malone and Bubba Midnight, Behind The Old Depot

"This better be important Malone," Bubba ranted, "because I had a good thing goin'."

"How bad do you want that money?"

"I got big plans with my share of the dough."

"I don't recall you giving me the account of the mineral rights, you 'dug up', and shall we say, about The Shady Rest Funeral Home."

"I put it in with all those other papers you had, you know, in that tan brief-case."

"I didn't see it…or find it, Bubba."

"Look man, you were at the funeral home, with Rose. You got up and went to the bathroom. Rose said she was gonna talk to Maudelle and I got a call from….well, never mind who, and I had to take it on the front porch. It was better reception out there."

"Well, it's not in there, Bubba."

"You reckon Rose took it?"

"I don't want to believe that."

"Look man, if that's all you wanted to ask me…."

"Bubba, keep your eyes open, cause things are going to start happening and happening fast! I won't be able to cover you…."

"I get the picture Malone. The minute my share conies in, I'm heading for Jamaica!'

"Yeah," Tom sighed. "Those little umbrella drinks are going to be quite tasty with…."

Bubba winked. "It's okay, like I said, I get the picture!"

CHAPTER 55

Dr. Marcus Donald and Sheriff Travis In Washington, D.C.

Dr. Donald gave the Sheriff a big grin, while glancing out the airline window at the Washington Monument. "I'm glad that our friend, Bea Winslow suggested you accompany me back to the big city. We probably won't have time to visit any of the attractions."

"That's okay, sir," replied Jim, "I've been to D.C. before. In fact, a number of times."

Marcus continued, "I've already phoned ahead and set up several appointments with our Senators. They have been diligently vetoing this thing ever since it arrived. Not to change the subject, but I am. You like Ms. Winslow, don't you?"

"Excuse me sir?" asked Jim.

"I was talking about Ms. Winslow, Bea."

"Yes…yes I do."

"A long time ago, she was engaged to my brother. He was killed in the Gulf War."

"I didn't know that."

"Few people did. She'll probably tell you in her own time. Well, here we are. After we land and retrieve our luggage, we'll go to my house.'

As they approached the brick colonial house, two golden Labradors came running from around the white picket fence.

"That's Sammy and Tinker. We've had them since they were puppies. And that's my wife Marcie, standing in the doorway."

"Hi ya, hon," Marcus said, while giving her a quick smooch. "This is Sheriff Jim Travis of Lafouchfeye County, Mississippi. You know," he laughed, "the one that Tate talks about so much."

"Very happy to meet you Sheriff. Dear, the Senator just called to check if you were back in town. He said it was urgent and to please call him."

Mr. Donald interrupted, "If you two will excuse me, I'd better contact the Senator."

"Thank you, Mrs. Donald for putting me up, on such short notice." "No problem, Sheriff. How's my good friend, Bea?"

"Please, call me Jim," he quickly replied. Bea......Bea is fine."

"Jim," smiled Marcie, "do you work with Bea a lot?"

"Yes ma'am. We have solved a number of crimes over the past several years."

"I know with all these 'important' things, Marcus has forgotten, but we made a commitment to attend Ford Theatre this evening and I hope you don't mind, but I've taken the liberty to have you escort my niece, Sally. It's just an obligatory thing, you understand. I believe Marcus has an extra tux you can borrow."

Jim paused and noticed Dr. Donald was motioning him to the phone. "Jim, you have a call....from Bea."

"Hello there! We just got in. Anything happening? Not much here, but this evening I have to escort Mrs. Donald's niece to a shindig at Ford's Theatre. Yeah....1 remember, that's where Lincoln was shot. Now, Bea...yes...I recall what you said. Don't worry, I'm safe. Yeah, sure I do. Take care. Bye now." After he hung up, he stood there with a smirk across his face.

"Everything okay?" asked Marcus.

"Huh? Oh sure....sure. She was just telling me I had eleven more to go......before I return to Lafouchfeye County."

The look on Marcus' face was evident he didn't understand.

"It's okay, Marcus.....just a inside joke....between Bea and I."

CHAPTER 56

Back In Lafouchfeye County
With Bea Winslow

Bea couldn't sleep. No, she wasn't thinking about her conversation with Jim, although she secretly hoped he would be able to work a little magic while he was in D.C.; no, it was her concern about Aunt Jewels. She was wondering where she was and how she was. Bea stared at the small stand that held the decorated Christmas tree with twinkling lights. Her Aunt had placed it on the windowsill just ten days ago. Aunt Jewels was always jubilant about the holidays! Bea laughed out loud as she recalled that evening when she approached her bedroom door, opened it and saw the little tree.

Turning around, Bea shouted down the stairs, "Aunt Jewels?"

"Yes dear?"

"Just what was your purpose of putting a Christmas tree in my bedroom? Correct me if I'm wrong, but I do believe you have a small hint of Christmas in every room of this house, including the garage!"

Aunt Jewels giggled as she started skipping up the polished wooden staircase. Now slightly out of breath, she paused at the top landing. "Excuse me? It's Christmas time. I thought you'd realize by now, I love to decorate during the holiday season. I noticed your room was bare…so I remedied that."

"But Aunt Jewels…I really don't need elves in my bathtub or angels holding my toothbrush."

"Maybe not dear, but as long as you live in my house, there will be lots of Christmas traditions!" With a sly wink, Aunt Jewels turned and seemingly floated down the stairs singing *"Angels We Have Heard On High."*

As Bea brushed a tear from her cheek, she muttered to herself, "Oh, dear Aunt Jewels, how I wish I could hear your senseless chatter, and I will soon, you hear? I promise!"

Just then her phone rang.

CHAPTER 57

Washington D.C., Early Morning of December 23rd

As the black limousine darted through the early morning traffic, Mr. Donald's eyes sparkled. "I have a fantastic idea! Barney," he informed the driver, "let's stop at that quaint little donut shop on the corner of Connecticut and Fifth Street. My dear, Barney and I have discovered a delightful goldmine! Haven't we Barney?"

"Sure have Mr. D."

"Marcus," his wife Marcie replied, "maybe Mr. Travis and certainly my niece, Sally, would like to retire for the rest of the evening, or should I say 'at this wee hour'. Both of them have been up nearly twenty-four hours."

Mr. Donald leaned forward. "Jim, you don't mind do you?"

Sheriff Travis looked at the two ladies and slowly shook his head from side to side.

"See, I told you Marcie! Good, we're almost there!"

About twenty minutes later, Barney parked the black sleek car next to the curb, got out and opened the rear door. As Mr. Donald stepped on the snowy sidewalk, his call phone beeper went off. He rolled his eyes upward, retrieved his phone and instantly recognized the number. It was the Senator. "Hello? Yes...I see...Yes sir, I understand. I realize the urgency. Yes, I will do that immediately. Yes sir, be careful."

Marcie watched her husband's face and became worried. "Marcus, is everything all right?"

"Well folks, we have a change of plans. Barney, drive us home, but keep the car running. Jim, that was our Senator. They have secretly passed the bill that these unscrupulous people want, you know, about the land deal. In reality however, they did this to flush out all the crooks. You, my friend, have to hi-tail it back to Lafouchfeye County and round them up from your end. That's where the danger lies. When they realize they have been hoodwinked, well as they say, the fur will fly!"

Jim took a deep breath. "Mr. Donald, may I borrow your cell phone and call Bea, so she can pick me up at the airport."

"Sure thing, son."

"Marcus...."

"Yes, my dear?"

"Sally, my niece, will be staying with us."

"Well, here we are. Jim, you go change and grab your suitcase. I'll wait for you in the car."

CHAPTER 58

At The End Of The Pier On East Beach, Near Citizen Street

Bubba nervously dialed Jeannie's number and then began waiting for her to answer.

"Hello? Oh….hi. Nothing, why? Now? Where's that Gerald Character? Because! Look Bubba, I won't go anywhere with you 'til I finish with him. You got that? Okay……I'll meet you near the water's edge, right after you drive across the Bay bridge. Turn right. Bye."

Now, as he looked at his cell phone, he could tell the charge was very, very low. Suddenly he remembered and pulled out the phone card he had received! Boy, oh boy. Now he could finish his phone calls. At this time of the morning, all the streets were deserted. Bubba parked his car and ducked into the half hidden phone booth.

Meathead coughed. "Hello? Who's this? Oh, yeah….what is it? You don't say!"

Mousy propped himself up on one elbow. "Who is it Meathead?"

He whispered, "Bubba."

"Who are you talkin' to Meathead?" Bubba questioned.

"Just Mousy, don't get your panties in a wad! No joke, it was passed? Who told ya? Sooooooo, when are we gettin' our share? Okay, okay, I hear ya! Naw, everyone is sleepin' like babies. Gotcha!"

"Meathead, what's up?"

"Mousy, you and me will soon be livin' it up in Mexico! That land deal went through and that Malone fella should be deliverin' the cash by tomorrow."

"Hey Meathead, you know what I wanta do? I wanta get my ma a nice present."

"Mousy, your ma's been dead two years now."

"I know, I know. I want to get her a pretty angel grave stone, you know, with big wings."

Meathead started rubbin' Mousy's shoulder. "That's a....nice thought."

At first when Aunt Jewels heard voices, she thought she was dreaming. Then she realized it was Mousy and Meathead talking, so she crawled over to the door and pressed her ear against the tiny crack. Obviously they were happy about something. Could this mean, she, the Doctor and his son, Amos, plus Maggie May would be set free? Or......no, she wouldn't even think like that! Quickly she scrambled back to where Dr. Banks was lying.

"Dr Banks......wake up."

"What is it Aunt Jewels?"

"I heard voices and thought I was dreaming, but I wasn't. Those two hood-lums out there received some kind of news. Something is going to happen."

Amos stirred beneath his shabby blanket. "What's goin' on?"

Dr. Banks whispered, "Aunt Jewels overheard our jailers talking and she believes a change is in the air."

Amos started shaking. "Oh mercy! They're gonna kill us!" he whimpered.

Aunt Jewels gritted her teeth. "Get a hold of yourself Amos! Nobody said anything about dying!"

"Well, you're an old fool if you think you're gonna walk outta here."

"I may be an old fool, but I believe we can over power those two. What do you think Doc?"

CHAPTER 59

At Bea And Aunt Jewel's House

The ringing phone startled Bea, as she laid in her bed, watching the twinkling lights on the small Christmas tree. She didn't recognize the return number and hesitated a minute before answering it. Slowly she lifted the receiver. "Hello? Mac! Where on earth are you? Really......I didn't know that number. No, no I wasn't asleep. Why? What have you found out? That's great! I knew he would take the bait! No, I haven't heard from Jim yet. Of course you're right. Call me the minute you receive a fixed address, Mac, and thanks again." Bea was beginning to feel more confident that Aunt Jewels and Maggie May would soon be found.

Once more the phone began ringing. "That was quick! What have you found out? Oh Jim! No, no, I thought it was Mac calling back. His contacts told him that Bubba Cuevas had used the phone card. When do you arrive and where? No problem, I'll be waiting." As she hung up the phone, Bea thought she heard a faint click. Could someone be in the house and listening on the kitchen phone? Her heart was pounding so; she thought it would jump out of her chest. Quietly she grabbed her revolver from the bedside table and slipped out of bed, her ears listening for any little sound. After slowly creeping toward the bedroom door, Bea proceeded to the top of the stairs. All seemed still and serene below. Hugging the left side of the wall, she carefully took one step at a time, until she was on the first landing. The shadows from Aunt Jewel's multicolored wheel, placed on the dining room table, created a kaleidoscope of circling images. Then she noticed a figure crouched behind the kitchen chair and the door wide open. She moved quickly, shouting, "Stay there or I'll shoot!"

They fled out the door and down the driveway. By the time Bea reached the back porch, she saw the car speeding away, but they had left a clue behind.

CHAPTER 60

Gerald Sheppard

Gerald Sheppard was quite disturbed, when he failed to reach Tom Malone at his motel room. Once more he dialed Tom's cell phone number. Nothing! He immediately tried to reach Bubba Cuevas. No answer! Where was everybody? Suddenly his cell phone rang. "Hello? Good, it's you, Bubba. What? When? How do you know this? You only heard half of the conversation? Did she see you? Are you sure? Do you know where Tom Malone is? Look, I'll be there on the next flight. We have to move and move fast! I'll go to the bank later this morning and get the money. We'll meet underneath the pier at Coleman Avenue around seven tonight. When you to contact Mousy and Meathead, here's what I want you to tell them…"

CHAPTER 61

The Old Barber Place

Because of the sharp chill in the air, Rose Fletcher pushed the fur collar of her mink coat up tightly around her neck. She had followed his orders impeccably; making sure no one had seen her leave the funeral home. Now making her way around to the back of the house, she paused. Was that a twig or branch she heard snap? No......her imagination was working overtime.

"Psst! Over here Rose," he whispered while grabbing her arm.

Shifting her head from side to side, she answered, "are you sure it's safe out here?"

"Quite sure my dear."

"Have you heard from Washington, D.C. yet?"

"Indirectly. Gerald will be arriving later this morning. We're suppose to distribute the money this evening, and then we'll be on our way."

Rose snuggled close to his chest. "We've waited seven years for this."

That's correct and I want you to go back and pack a light suitcase. Just a few necessary things and meet me back here around 11:30 p.m."

"I will dear, and please take care. I want to share our time in Switzerland!"

After a long passionate kiss, Rose started walking towards the broken gate. However, having difficulty sliding through and bending down, she caught her silk scarf and it slid from around her neck. Unaware of her loss, she continued towards her car, parked in a grove of pecan trees, by the side of the road.

From out of the shadows, came the figure of a woman. "Now, that was quite touching," she smirked.

Although startled, he maintained his composure. "How long have you been there?"

"She gave a throaty laugh. "Long enough."

"Then you realize I was just playing her along."

"Do I?"

"Of course."

"And why should I trust and believe you?"

"Because we have had a mutual attraction for the same thing all along. Money."

"You are so right my love," and slowly advanced towards him until she was nestled between his arms in a passionate embrace.

At the car, Rose noticed her scarf was missing and retraced her steps. In the moonlight, she saw the two of them, wrapped in each other's arms.

CHAPTER 62

Bea Winslow, At Home

After closing the kitchen door, Bea hurried back up to her bedroom and retrieved her cell phone. "Hello, Deputy Paulie, this is Bea Winslow. No, no I'm okay, but Bubba Cuevas broke into my house a few minutes ago. No, I didn't see him exactly, just his form, crouched behind my kitchen chair. However, he dropped his cell phone in my driveway. If you dust the kitchen phone, you'll find his fingerprints on it. Yes, sure thing. I'll wait here for you. Yes, I did. I'm picking the Sheriff up in an hour at the Gulfport/Biloxi International Airport. See you in a few minutes."

After closing her cell phone, she decided on making a cup of tea. Soon the whistling teakettle got her attention. She was surprised when the kitchen phone began ringing. She couldn't pick it up, so she quickly ran upstairs to answer her bedroom phone. "Hello? Who is this? Why do you think I'd be interested? I see......go on. And why do you believe that? No, no, I am interested, very interested. Why are you telling me all of this? You would be willing to testify? Hello? Hello?" The line was dead.

As Bea looked out the bedroom window, she saw Deputy Paulie's patrol car pulling off the main road. Quickly she changed into her jeans and a sweatshirt, and then hurried downstairs.

"I saw your headlights," smiled Bea.

"I noticed when I pulled into the driveway," Deputy Paulie chuckled, "Bubba must have backed his car onto the driveway, and because he cut the edge short and almost took out your Aunt's corner gardenia bush!"

"Yes, he was in a hurry. He thought I was going to shoot him!"

"Now let me have a look at this phone. Oh, Ms Bea, look at this. Here is a good clear one. Looks like he was eatin' chocolate. That's a perfect thumb print, if I ever saw one."

"That's not the only thing. I bet he not only listened in on my phone, but also used it to call his buddies. You see, I arranged it so he received a phone card that he could use instead of his cell phone."

Deputy Paulie's face broke into a broad grin. "That's a neat idea!"

"Well," Bea confessed, "it wasn't an original; I had read about it, so I figured, why not?"

"Has it worked?"

"Sure has. Mac called me earlier. He's got his resources running the trace. Oh yes, I just received a very interesting phone call. Although the voice was muffled, I believe it was a woman. You know what she said?"

"What….Ms. Winslow?"

"She mentioned that Horace Fletcher was alive."

With that remark, Deputy Paulie stopped brushing the phone receiver, turned, and stared at Bea. "But he died, was shot seven years ago."

"Was he? Did you see the body? Oh my gosh! Look at the time. You stay here Deputy, I have to pick up the Sheriff."

"You just want me to close and lock the door, Ms. Winslow?"

"Sure thing, see you later!"

CHAPTER 63

Mac Calls Bea And Sheriff Travis Arrives

Sitting at the airport, Bea nervously fidgeted with her purse, shuffling and flipping her case of contact cards. Suddenly her cell phone rang. "Hello? Mac....what have you found out now? Really? No, not yet. His plane is due in any minute. I've got some interesting news also. While I was still home, someone called me. Sounded like a woman trying to muffle her voice. She mentioned that Horace Fletcher was alive. That's correct. I said alive. Where are you at now? I see...well please be careful. Thanks for the information. Bye, now."

As Bea flipped the phone cover down, the overhead system announced Flight 7689 from Washington, D.C. was landing. Within twenty minutes, Bea noticed Jim trudging towards her, through the small crowd. The instant he cleared the plate glass door, his face broke into a wide grin. "Well now, a pretty woman and a smile. This is an almost perfect welcome home."

Bea slowly walked toward him, and then stopped. "I suppose you want a kiss?"

Jim rolled his eyes. "The thought crossed my mind."

Reaching her arms around his neck, Bea brushed his cheek, and then gazed into his eyes. "Don't get too confident, Sheriff Travis," she smirked, then pressed her lips firmly upon his.

"Well now Bea," he replied, a second later, "I'm tempted to re-create Ado Annies boyfriend in the show *'Oklahoma'*!"

Looking into his eyes, she questioned, "And what might that be?"

Jim boasted, "Well, when he saw Ado Annie again, after being in the big city, he stepped over her like this, grabbed her waist," and suddenly Jim plunged Bea toward the floor, directly in front of him. As she looked around, she saw an audience was gathering. Gazing into Jim's face, Bea had a perplexed look.

He smiled back. "This is called a 'hearty Oklahoma hello'!"

The crowd started applauding.

Bea's eyes twinkled. "I can tell you are excited to be back home in Mississippi."

Pulling Bea up to a standing position, Jim squeezed her waist. "Very much so Bea, very, very much!"

CHAPTER 64

Gerald Sheppard At The Bank

When Gerald couldn't reach Tom Malone, he became quite agitated. Where was he? He hadn't answered his cell or land phone for twenty-four hours. After talking to Meathead, Gerald made the decision to get rid of all the extra baggage. But that would come later, after he and his sweetie were in Switzerland. Now he had to concentrate on getting all the funds.

As he approached the Bank's front door, he glanced about, making sure of his surroundings. Good…only a few people were nearby, therefore he didn't notice Sheriff Travis standing across the street at the gas station, bent over a car hood supposedly checking the oil.

He smiled, while strolling over by the receptionist's desk.

"Good morning sir, Merry Christmas! How can I be of service to you?"

"You are so correct! Just two more days. I'm overwhelmed by your pleasantness. I do wish to converse with Mr. Porter, the Bank Manager. Is he in yet?"

As she glanced towards the glassed-in office, she saw it was empty. "I'm sure he's in sir. I'll check in the back."

"Thank you."

Again she smiled. "Please, have a seat."

As she disappeared around the rear corner, Tom Malone came barging thru the front doors. Not wanting to appear alarmed, Gerald stood there, grinning from ear to ear. "Why hello Tom, why are you here?"

Frustrated, Tom replied, "You were supposed to call me."

"Please, calm yourself. Let's discuss this. Now," Gerald added discreetly, "I tried to contact you by both lines, but couldn't. Where have you been?"

"That doesn't matter right now. Have you talked to the Bank Manager yet?"

"No, the receptionist has summoned him."

"Look, we have a problem."

"No Tom, we don't, you do."

"No…., we do! Horace Fletcher is alive!"

Gerald's face registered shock. "What do you mean…alive? He died seven years ago. You told me…"

Just then the cheery receptionist returned with Mr. Porter scurrying behind her. "Here he is, Mr…."

"Sheppard, Mr. Gerald Sheppard."

"Oh I see someone else has joined you. Will he be seeing Mr. Porter also?"

"No, my friend has other business to take care of." Facing Tom, Gerald added, "I suggest you check that out thoroughly and get back to me."

"This way Mr. Sheppard," the receptionist replied, "Mr. Porter is waiting for you."

CHAPTER 65

Maudelle Confronts Charlie

Several days had gone by since Maudelle had caught Charlie standing by the barn and talking on his cell phone to a woman! Since then, he had made sure he stayed confined to his wheelchair. Now, sitting on the front porch swing, Maudelle was steady staring in Charlie's direction.

"What's up sugar?" he asked. "You look like you have somethin' on your mind. Are you wonderin' what I got you for Christmas?"

"Not really, Charlie," she drawled. "Just thinkin' how things would have turned out, if you could still walk."

Charlie let out a boisterous laugh. "Yeah…I've pondered on that one myself, but not here lately." As he patted his hands on each side of the tires, he remarked, "guess I've finally resigned my thinkin' to sittin' here for the rest of my life."

Maudelle leaned forward and said, "And just how long is that, Charlie?"

"Okay, Maudelle, what's gnawin' in your craw?"

Maudelle pushed her feet down on the porch, causing the swing to begin swaying. "Nothin' is gnawin' me in any place, Charlie."

"Well, somethin's wrong. Is it because Pearl, Timmy or I haven't helped you keep the house clean?"

"That could be, Charlie. You know I could always use some extra hands."

"Well sugar, if you'd like, I can get them folks to clean up a little more than they do."

"Charlie, what would you do if I wasn't around?"

"What'ya mean?"

"You know….if I was to leave….again."

"Gosh Maudelle, I don't know……I really don't know. You ain't planning nothin' like that, are you?"

"No Charlie, I'm not, but if I ever catch you messin' around anybody or find out anything that's not true….well, let's just say your life in that wheelchair is over."

Charlie let out a heavy sigh. "Sugar," he said sweetly, while rolling over to the swing, "Sugar, you can always count on me and you know it."

Maudelle looked him straight in his eyes. "Charlie, that sounds like a good idea, because if it isn't, your bones may be the ones they'll dig up twenty years from now!"

CHAPTER 66

Tom Malone Is Surprised

When Tom checked his cell phone messages, he didn't like what he saw. She had called four times. Shrugging his shoulders, he reluctantly redialed her number. "You called? Yeah…yeah, I know he's back. That's right, he's getting the money at this very moment. What do you mean? No! Where's the car now? I see. She's not that good. I just know, that's why! Look, you know the plan! Now, let me go and I'll see you later. That's correct. I have another call. Bye. Hello? What? Yes…yes…where are they now? Okay Bubba. Bye."

As Tom closed his cell phone, he believed he saw a shadow pass by the window of his motel room. Cautiously, he moved toward the door. Suddenly a small rap caused him to freeze. Who could it be?

"Yes? He answered.

"Tom?" came her reply.

Instantly, he jerked open the metal painted door. There stood his wife, Crissy.

"I thought I'd surprise you!" She grinned.

CHAPTER 67

Mousy and Meathead

Things had been quiet for several hours at the run down shack off of high-way 603. Meathead pushed back his ragged sleeve. His watch read eleven o'clock.

"Mousy?" He whispered.

"Yeah? What's up?"

"You are. It's almost dinner time."

"Gosh, Meathead, is it that late?"

"No stupid, not supper…lunch."

"Oh…"

"Yeah…here's some dough. Take the car, and follow the back roads over to that little cafe and pick up some food for our guests."

"Hey, Meathead, have you heard from Bubba again?"

"Why?"

"Just wonderin'."

"Look, just do what I asked you to do, and be careful. We're takin' a chance goin' out in the day time, but I figure it may be their last meal."

"Meathead….you mean we're gonna….?"

"Mousy, just get the food, I'm hungry!"

Mousy didn't mind being the gopher. He enjoyed the outdoors. Why, when he was growin' up, his old man use to take him fishin' and huntin', before he went to Parchman. When he met Meathead in the county jail, he sorta latched onto him like a clamp. Now as he drove down the dusty road, he spied an old farmhouse on the right. Christmas lights were strung across the grey picket fence. Geez, he thought, Christmas is only two days away.

The turn in the road led him directly to the small cafe. Mousy hopped out of the pick up truck and dug deep in his pocket, pulling out all the money Meathead had given him.

Parked at the opposite corner and slightly hidden by several stacks of barrels, were Officer Barney Frye and Officer Maddie Trace.

"Well, have you decided what you want to eat?" Asked Barney.

"What are you getting?" she questioned.

"Oh I was thinking of a BLT on toast, with fries and a coke."

"That sounds good to me. You ready to go in?"

"Sure enough. Got to keep track of the time though. Remember, I'm meeting with that Detective, Barry Luce."

When they entered the cafe, Mousy had already placed his order to go and was sittin' in the booth, closest to the jukebox.

"Well," grinned Mabel, the chubby waitress, "if it ain't Bay St. Louis' finest. Tweedledum and Tweedledee. What brings you out in these parts?"

"Why you Mabel," laughed Barney. "I told Officer Trace here, all about your BLT's and she had to have one!"

After the laughter died down, both Officer's noticed the unkempt little man sitting in the rear booth.

"Sir?" Mabel shouted. "Sir?"

Mousy looked up.

"Your food is ready."

As Mousy approached the counter, he lowered his head.

"Hi there," replied Officer Barney. "Haven't I seen you before?"

"No....no, don't believe so. I don't live around these parts."

"Is that your pick up outside?" Asked Officer Trace.

"No, it belongs to a friend of mine."

"Well, tell your friend, his inspection sticker will run out the end of this month."

"Thanks, I'll do that. Bye, ma'am."

After Mousy had pulled out, he slowly made his way back down the rutted road.

Barney kept watching the pick up truck until it disappeared around the bend. "Wait a minute! Maddie, I remember him now. He was locked up about a month ago. Petty larceny. Him and a heavy set dude."

CHAPTER 68

Mac Meets With Bea and Sheriff Travis

As Bea pulled up to the Sheriffs office, she noticed Mac's Volvo was nowhere in sight. Where was he? She no sooner thought those words and up he drove, parking on the left side of the Sheriffs jeep.

"Sorry I'm late," he apologized. "I was talking to the Bridge Master."

"What about?"

"I'll fill you both in when we get inside."

While opening the door, they saw Sheriff Travis on the phone. "Yeah Barney......where? No, I understand. Sure....well let me know how that meeting goes. Bye."

"Anything important?" Bea questioned.

Sheriff Travis lowered his head, while shuffling papers around on the top of his desk.

"Jim?"

"Well Bea, you remember that little cafe that sits way back in the woods off of highway 603?"

"Yes, what about it?"

"We ate there once. It's run by Mabel Cuevas."

"Jim?"

"Barney and Officer Trace stopped there for a bite to eat. There was a wiry little man waiting for a take-out order. Barney looked at him once or twice, but couldn't make the connection. When Mabel told him his large order was ready, he thanked her and left. After he had driven down the road, Barney remembered where he had seen him. At the county jail locked up for petty larceny. Him and a hefty fat dude."

"You mean to tell me, he possibly could have tracked him back to Where Aunt Jewels is being kept and didn't?"

"No Bea, he tried tailing him, but he lost him after several turns."

Bea threw up her hands in disgust and then slumped into the stained ladder back chair.

"I'm sorry Bea…"

"Jim, you realize we haven't much time left. You know as well as I do, once they get that money and divide it, they'll kill any hostages they have left!"

"Look, I knew Gerald Sheppard would go to the bank this morning, once he had been notified the phony bill had been passed. I got there early and laid out our plan to the receptionist and Mr. Porter, the Bank Manager. Sure enough, right at nine o'clock, Sheppard entered the bank. Tom Malone also showed up. He didn't stay long, however. Since it was a large withdrawal, Mr. Porter asked Sheppard to return around five o'clock. Bea, trust me, we'll find Aunt Jewels and that dog. Mac, what have you found?"

"Well mates, my sources tell me Mr. Bubba Cuevas has been calling everybody, so we know getaway plans are definitely in the works. They're still working on several locations though."

"Okay Mac, what about the Bridge Master?"

He grinned. "You know mates, you never realize where you will find a gold nugget. The Bridge Master is a lady by the name of Lucille Tinsley."

Bea rolled her eyes. "So?"

"So….my dear Bea, Lucille was on duty the night a rather large vessel decided to dump some wrapped up cargo overboard."

"And you're telling me she can identify the boat and the people?"

"Yep! Lucille said they hang out at The Firedog Saloon and The Paper Moon."

CHAPTER 69

Officer Barney Frye Meets With Detective Barry Luce

After he had dropped off Officer Maddie Trace, Barney rushed over to Stennis Space Center and his appointment with Detective Barry Luce. He had completed his research, plus his Uncle, Dr. Nathan Tate and Dr. Marcus Donald of Washington, D.C. had sent him fax's and e-mails concerning Mr. Luce and his dealings. Sheriff Travis, Mac Tavis and Ms. Bea had been helpful also.

As Barney slowly drove through the checkpoint, he thought back to his initial meeting with Detective Luce and his three fellow agents. Were they agents? Yes, both he and Dr. Donald had run a check on their authenticity and all three had passed the grade. No, Barney was convinced Detective Barry Luce was working alone.

Now parking in the reserved spot for security, he quickly moved toward the building and Detective Luce's office on the fifth floor. Barney's nostrils couldn't help but smell the sweet scent of jasmine &he stepped into the elevator. The aroma continued down the hall and into the outer office of Detective Barry Luce.

Approaching Miss Penny, the receptionist, Barney remarked, "That's a lovely cologne you are wearing."

She blushed and replied, "That's not mine. Detective Luce had a lady visitor earlier."

Noticing Miss Penny wasn't wearing a ring, Barney grinned, and replied, "well then, maybe you should buy a small bottle. Sure smells good!"

Once more she blushed and giggled.

As Barney looked around for a magazine, he spied a paisley silk scarf lying on the floor, underneath a chair. Picking it up, he ambled over to her desk. "Is this yours?"

"Why no. Where did you find it?"

Barney pointed toward the right corner. "Under that chair."

"Oh….it must be hers."

"Hers?" Barney questioned.

"Detective Luce's friend."

"I….see."

At that precise moment, the huge walnut door to his office swung open and Detective Barry Luce sauntered out. He looked at Officer Frye and smirked. "Thinking of adding a scarf to your uniform?"

"Oh, this? No, I just found it, over there, under that chair."

"Miss Penny, would you mind keeping it? I'll give her a call later. Now, Officer Frye, how can I help you?"

"Well sir, I would like to go over the initial burglary and assault sheet you wrote up on Maggie May's Gift Shop in Bay St. Louis. True, I've read it over and over, but I would like a one on one, personal account."

"No problem. Have a seat in front of my desk. Miss Penny, we do not want to be disturbed."

"Yes sir," replied Officer Frye, but instead he walked over to the opposite wall that held a huge map of the entire Stennis Space Center. For some reason, his eyes scanned the right side and came to rest on a small faded black dot.

When the massive door closed, Officer Frye could feel Detective Luce's eyes penetrate his entire body. This was a dangerous man and Barney was going to remain cool. Turning around, he asked, "Detective Luce, do you know a Dr. Marcus Donald?"

"Marc?" In Washington, D.C.? Sure do. We've worked a few cases together. Good man Marc."

"Well then, are you familiar with the land bill that has just been pushed through and signed, extending the perimeter of Stennis Space Center up to and including the outer limits of Bay St. Louis and Lafouchfeye County?"

"Really, Officer Frye, I'm head of National Security here at Stennis. Of course I'm aware of such an action." Luce was curious about him looking at the map.

"Of course you realize," continued Officer Frye, "Mr. Tom Malone has bought all the property adjacent to the land in question…"

Detective Luce interrupted, "I believe he hasn't purchased The Shady Rest Funeral Home parcel and probably won't."

"And why not?"

"Because Rose, I mean Mrs. Fletcher isn't going to sell. By the way, you looked like you were interested in my map. Did you notice something?"

Barney heard him, but moved his body forward. "According to my facts and figures, several gentlemen are going to make a pretty nickel."

"It's more than a nickel, Officer Frye."

"That was just a figure of speech. Excuse me sir, have you managed to acquire any leads to the whereabouts of Mrs. Julia McKenna, Doctor Horatio Banks, his son, Amos Seals and the dog called Maggie May?"

"Officer Frye, I believe I gave my information to Sheriff Jim Travis. In fact, Mr. Travis and I talked several days ago."

Barney politely moved his chair back and stood up. "Detective Luce, I believe you also had a meeting with Mr. Mac Tavis, but anyway, I want to thank you for this opportunity."

Barry Luce's smile was more like a sneer. My mistake, Officer Frye," he replied, while rising from his comfortable chair. "Anytime I can be of service to the local police, but you haven't answered my question."

Barney turned and started for the door. "Question? There is one more thing."

"And that is?" Replied Detective Luce.

"I understand you sold the Fletcher's a 1927 Model T. Ford."

"Many years ago, during a *Cruisin' The Coast* event."

"Well, Detective Luce, it might surprise you to find out that Mr. Horace Fletcher is alive!"

"Officer Frye, I do believe your necktie is a bit tight. Horace Fletcher died seven years ago. Now if you'll excuse me, I have some rather important calls to return, after you answer my question."

"And that was?"

"Did you see anything on the map? You looked at it with much interest."

"Oh, I was noticing where the old weighing station was and how the new highway was miles away from it."

"Really."

CHAPTER 70

The Rescue of Aunt Jewels and Maggie May

When Mac, Bea and Sheriff Travis arrived at the Backwoods Cafe, the same one Barney called the Sheriff about, Mabel, the owner was about to close.

"Well howdy folks, you're a little late."

"Mabel, I'm Sheriff Travis, from Lafouchfeye County and this is Bea Winslow, a Private Investigator and our friend Mac Tavis."

Mabel chuckled to herself, then let out a yowl like laughter. "For goodness sakes Sheriff, I remember you and the little lady. It hasn't been that long ago." Looking long and hard at Mac Tavis, she moved a little closer to him and rested her hands on both hips. "Now you mister, I haven't seen in these here parts. What did you say your name was?"

"Tavis, Mac Tavis, from the F.B.I, out of Washington, D.C."

"Mercy! Okay Sheriff, what in tarnation is takin' place now?"

"Well, Mabel, Officer Barney Frye......"

"Yeah, he was here earlier...this afternoon. Him and a little police lady had lunch. He also tore outa here, chasin' somebody, and then came back to eat."

"Well ma'am, that's why we're here."

"You wanted to see where he ate?"

"No Mabel, we wanted to ask you if you recalled the other fella that you sold the takeout food to."

"Oh him. Scrawny little varmint. Reminded me of a mouse.
Could have used a bath, if you know what I mean."

The Sheriff rubbed his fingers across his chin and asked, "Have you seen him before, you know around these parts?"

"Yeah, he's come in several times and picked up drinks and cold sandwiches. One time however," Mabel's face brighten up, "he had me fix breakfast," and started counting on her fingers. "For seven people. Oops…make that six people and a dog. Now that was a good ticket!"

Bea's eyes lit up. "A dog?"

"Yeah……he said he was gonna give the pooch a good breakfast."

"Mabel, you don't happen to know which way he left from here do you?" Asked Mac.

Again she gave him a dubious look. "Well now little fella, he took off down that dirt road," and pointed toward the left corner of the building.

Mac took a quick gander towards that direction, but asked, "why not to the right, Mabel?"

Once more she let out a loud yowl. "You don't know nothin' about these here parts, do you son? That old road leads to a deserted shack back in the woods, off of highway 603. It used to be a weighing station, but then the highway got moved. Yeah, I had some hi-falootin men come around here, a few months back. They thought my property was important! Well, I contacted my nephew on my pappy's side, and Tom straightened 'em out real fast like!"

Mac, Bea and the Sheriff glanced at each other, and then the Sheriff asked, "Are you speaking of Tom Malone, the Highway Superintendent?"

"Sure enough. You know him?"

Bea smiled, "yes ma'am, we know him."

"Well then, maybe he can help you out," winked Mabel.

Just then Bea's cell phone rang.

Mabel started cackling. "Those little things are so cute!"

"Hello?" Bea replied. "Yes, as a matter of fact we are nearby. Thanks for the information. Where are you now? Yes……yes…okay, see you there. That was Barney……he just saw Luce……and he discovered the old weighing station."

As Mac and the Sheriff were listening to Bea, Mac's cell phone jangled.

Mabel developed a deep frown on her face. She just wasn't too sure of this new guy.

"Yeah!" Mac answered quickly. That's great! Thanks a lot! Bea, they got a match! That has to be the place!"

The Sheriff quickly grabbed Mabel's hand and began pumping it. "Thanks for your time and trouble Ms. Mabel, but we must be going."

"Come back anytime for vittles, you hear?" And then stared at Mac, as he too, turned to leave. "Even you there."

"Thanks, matey!" He replied.

"What'cha call that?" Mabel asked.

Bea laughed. "He's Scottish and Australian, Mabel, he was just saying 'howdy-do'!"

"Oh......see ya!"

"She is a character, isn't she?" Bea snickered, while poking Jim Travis in the back.

"Bea, I want you to ride with Mac. I have to return to Bay St. Louis," remarked the Sheriff.

"What do you mean? We're this close to possibly finding Aunt Jewels and you're leaving?"

"Bea, Gerald Sheppard is suppose to meet with Mr. Porter at five. Trust me...I'll be in touch. What I'm hoping is that Sheppard meets with Malone and Bubba, to give them their share. Remember, we have to be careful. Luce is a dangerous man. If he gets just a small inkling of what's going on, it could turn nasty."

"I should realize by now, that nailing the bad guys is the hardest part."

"That's my girl...now you and Mac travel down that dirt road and meet Barney. He's already cased out the shack."

"You be careful Jim, remember you're dealing with a man who burned down a house and killed his girlfriend."

CHAPTER 71

The Sting: A Rose Among Thorns

While sitting on the back deck of The Dock of the Bay restaurant, waiting for his appointment with Mr. Porter, the Bank Manager, Gerald Sheppard slowly sipped his coffee and thought of his upcoming trip to Switzerland. Pushing his sleeve back, he saw it was almost five o'clock.

First, he would collect the money and then notify Tom. Afterwards he would call Bubba and tell him to inform Mousy and Meathead to the termination of all the hostages. Everything was coming together and working beautifully.

Suddenly his thoughts were interrupted by a sweet voice. "Can I get you another cup of coffee, sir?" asked the waitress.

Gerald looked up into a set of gorgeous blue eyes. "Why no, ma'am, but thank you anyway." He watched her as she strolled away. Now it was time to go. I'll leave her a generous tip, he mused to himself. She's probably putting herself through college.

As he nonchalantly moved to the bar and headed toward the front entrance, he was completely unaware of the young lady in a light tan linen jacket, falling in step behind him. Once outside, he had to wait for several vehicles to pass before he could cross the street to the bank. Just as he reached for the bank door handle, he felt something jab his rib cage.

"That's a good boy, Gerald," she whispered. "Just keep right on moving."

That voice…it was the waitress…

"No Gerald, don't make any sudden moves. Just do as I say…"

Gerald interrupted her, "I know the routine little lady and no one gets hurt."

"I'm sure you do. Ah….there's Mr. Porter, coming to greet us.

"Mr. Sheppard and Mrs. Sheppard I presume."

"Yes sir, the little woman has to be involved in something this important!"

"Well, Mr. Sheppard, I've managed to gather all the funds you have requested. Of course I will require a signed receipt. It's not often I have such a large amount. So much so I have had to 'rob' our nearby branches."

While hanging on to Gerald's arm, the young lady replied, "Oh Gerald, I can hardly wait until we leave for Switzerland!"

Gerald Sheppard's head jerked to face her, and then he regained his composure. "Quiet, my dear, or you'll give away all our secrets!"

As Mr. Porter was placing the strapped money in the black valise, his desk phone began ringing.

"I didn't realize a banker was such a busy man," smiled Gerald.

"Hello, Mr. Porter here. Why yes….no, that's perfectly acceptable. No, I understand entirely. Goodbye." Looking at Mr. Sheppard, he replied, "that was my wife….she was just letting me know of our dinner reservations. Well, that about does it." As he stretched forth his hand……

"Oh Mr. Porter, I'm sorry but Gerald jammed his hand in our car door. I'm so sorry he cannot shake your hand," she said sweetly.

"That's okay ma'am. I've done the same thing. Hurt like hell…oh excuse me."

"Are you ready to go dear?" She asked.

"Anytime you are, since you're driving."

Mr. Porter watched from his office doorway; as they departed through the double front doors and then flipped open his cell phone. "Sheriff? He just left, but he had a woman with him. I think she had a gun and was poking him in his side. She was blonde, but it could have been a wig. Big blue eyes and slim figure. Oh, you see them? Great! That's right, it's all marked phony money. Sure, that's okay. Keep me posted. Right! Bye."

CHAPTER 72

Gerald Sheppard and Friend

As she pushed him across the car console, Gerald winched. "Watch it lady, my legs are longer than yours!"

"Just be thankful I didn't shoot them off!"

Am I supposed to know you?" he asked.

"Just drive. Call up your friend Tom Malone. Tell him you'll meet him at the old Winslow boathouse."

"Hell, that's forty miles from here!"

"Tell him!"

"Okay…okay, don't get slap happy with that rod!"

"I know Curtis, you never expected to see me again, but you never know about the future, do you?"

"You got the wrong man lady. My name is Sheppard, Gerald Sheppard."

"That's what you call yourself now, but your name was Curtis Burras. You don't remember me, do you? Let me refresh your memory. Your girlfriend picked up my brother and me, took us to the old house, fed us and got us drunk, only I didn't pass out.…so she put me in the front room. I heard your conversation and then you carried me outside and dumped me in the bushes and set the house on fire. You thought you killed me, but you missed."

"So…that's who you are."

"Yeah…..I'm Jeannie Rose. Bennie was my brother and you killed him!"

"Do you know how much money is in that valise? Lots! Leave me some, but take the rest. We don't have to share with anybody else!"

"What about your girlfriend, what's her name? Mrs. Tom Malone? Crissy? What about her and your trip to Switzerland?"

"You're just full of surprises, aren't you?"

"Just like you, Curtis, just like you," she smiled.

"Now I get it. That's why you wanted Tom to meet us away from Bay St. Louis. I suppose you told Crissy the same thing."

"Curtis, you are a fast learner."

Gerald/Curtis smiled. "It comes with the occupation."

"Well friend, we're almost there……and would you look at that. They're both inside."

Thirty Minutes Later

"That's right Curtis," Jeannie laughed. "Tie them up nice and tight."

Tom's eyes flashed and his words snapped at his wife Crissy. "You were going to leave with this sleaze bag?"

"Now, now, Mr. Malone," snickered Jeannie, "I certainly would be so quick to judge."

"And just what were you going to do, Mr. Macho man?" screamed Crissy.

"Well now," Jeannie Rose grinned, "you two have lot's of time to talk. Tom, here's your share of the money and when you get loose, y'all can battle it out. Bye now. Come on Curtis, we have to meet Bubba."

Waiting patiently at the top of the hill, were Sheriff Travis in his Jeep and two patrol cars. Deputy Paulie in one and Deputy Taylor in the other. As soon as Gerald/Curtis and the young lady left, Sheriff Travis and Deputy Paulie moved in toward the old boathouse. Deputy Taylor was tailing Gerald/Curtis.

"Well now, what have we here?" asked the Sheriff. "I believe it's Tom and Crissy Malone, correct? What we are going to do is keep you tied up and transport you out to Deputy Paulie's car. I'll take the money. See you back at the jail folks!"

Twenty Minutes Later Down the Road With
Gerald/Curtis and Jeannie

"Where to now?" Gerald/Curtis asked.

"Call Bubba."

"That number is no good. Won't go through."

"Use this one instead," Jeannie urged, handing him a sliver of paper.

"Hello?" replied a husky voice.

"Bubba?"

"Yeah…who is this?"

"Sheppard. Where are you?"

"I'm on my boat."

"I'm coming with your share of the money."

"Great!"

"Okay," whispered Jeannie, "hang up."

"Now what?" he asked.

"We leave Bubba his share, that's what."

"Then what happens?"

"We have to meet with Barry Luce," Jeannie added.

"Sweetheart, do you know who you're dealing with?"

"Is that supposed to frighten me?"

"Well, he has a lot to lose."

Deputy Taylor Radios Sheriff Travis

"Sheriff, they're headin' towards the short pier right off the right side of the bay bridge."

Sheriff Travis answered, "Bubba Cuevas has a boat slip there. That's who is meeting them. I, well I called Ms. Winslow about a young woman riding with Gerald Sheppard. She figured out what was going on. Jeannie Rose hijacked Gerald Sheppard. He killed her brother in that Vancleave road fire seven years ago."

"So…she's not in the money scheme?"

"No, it doesn't seem so. Keep your eyes and ears open though."

"Will do."

Gerald/Curtis And Jeannie Rose

"Come on….get out!" She ordered.

"Jeannie Rose!" Bubba yelled. "What the hell are you doing?"

"Bubba, I told you I was goin to take care of Mr. Sheppard/Burras first before anything else!"

"Yeah…but…."

"Well, no buts about it. Now here's your share of the money. Go ahead Gerald or Curtis. Tie him up!"

"Jeannie! I thought you were goin' to Jamaica with me? Why in the hell are you tiein' me up?"

"Well, you thought wrong! We need time to get away. Give me your cell phone."

"I don't have one….only this phone card."

"Thanks. Come on you, get back in the car. We have another stop!"

After they had pulled away, he glanced over at her. "Where to now?"

"As if you didn't know. Call Mr. Barry Luce. We'll meet him at the beach on the corner of Coleman Avenue and North Beach."

"Hey, it's me, Gerald. Are you ready for your share of the dough? Sure, sure, I'm looking at it now…..in the passenger seat. I've already taken care of the other two, Malone and Cuevas. That's right. Be there in twenty minutes."

"That was very good. No ulterior motives," smiled Jeannie.

"That offer's still good, you know? We can eliminate Luce and you can fly off to Europe."

"Nope……ain't gonna happen."

"So……it's not just me you're after."

"Shut up and drive."

CHAPTER 73

The Hideaway Off of Highway 603

"Mousy would you sit down and quit pacing back and forth? You're makin' me nervous!"

"Meathead, wasn't Bubba suppose to call us? When is he gonna call us?"

"Shut up and let me think!" He pulled out the little silver cell phone and punched in Bubba's numbers. Nothing. He tried it again. Still nothing. "Did you hear somethin'?"

Mousy stood stiff as a board. "No. Why?"

"I thought I heard somebody outside."

"Youze want me to check, Meathead?"

"Sure, why don't you do that."

Just as Mousy started for the door, Meathead jumped up! "Are you nuts or somethin'? If somebody or somethin' is out there, it just might grab you!"

"Ohhhhhhh…yeah, Meathead…youze is right."

Just then Meathead's cell phone rang. "Oh, hi, Mr. Luce. No kiddin'! That's good news! What? Now? If you say so. See you soon."

"Who was that Meathead?"

"Mr. Luce. He says we have to get rid of the people."

"You mean……turn them loose?"

"No, you dope…we have to 'get rid' of them…in other words kill'em. Here…take my gun and go do it."

Suddenly the front door crashed open! "Drop that gun, Meathead!" Yelled Officer Barney Frye.

Bea came running through, her pistol drawn. "Okay where's my Aunt Jewels?" She demanded.

Mousy was standing there shivering, pointin' his finger. "She's in the next room, ma'am. Her and the dog!"

"Shut up, Mousy!" yelled Meathead.

"You be quiet, yourself!" Officer Frye snapped, while cuffing Meathead's hands behind his back. "You're mighty lucky we found them alive!"

The wooden door didn't budge as Bea pushed against it. "Aunt Jewels!" She screamed. Maggie May began barking loudly.

"Bea! Bea! We're in here! They've locked the door!"

"Stand back Aunt Jewels! Get away from it! We're breaking it down! Come on Mac! Use your shoulder! One…two…three!"

In a split second, the rusted lock and casing splintered, sending it crashing to the floor. Bea would have gone down with the door, but Mac steadied her. "I'm fine now. Thanks Mac."

Maggie May darted between the two women and headed straight for Meathead.

"Bea dear," Aunt Jewels shouted, shaking her fist at Mousy and Meathead. "I told these hoodlums you would come, didn't I? You remember Dr. Banks, don't you?" And this is his son Mr. Banks Jr., and of course, Amos Seals. Mercy me. I almost forgot Maggie May. She has been such a sweet dog. Well would you look at that!" Come over here old girl, he's already been handcuffed!"

Dr. Horatio Banks stepped forward and grabbed Bea's hand. "Ms. Winslow, you really don't know how happy I am to see you!"

"You can thank Officer Barney Frye. He was the one who figured it out, plus Mac put a tail on Bubba's phone calls."

Mac grinned. "Bea, you're too modest. It was you who gave the phone card to Bubba in the first place, so we could trace his calls."

Aunt Jewels began looking around. "Where's that nice Sheriff?"

Bea winked at Mac. "I knew she'd ask."

"Well?" Aunt Jewels questioned.

"The good Sheriff," smiled Bea, "is rounding up all the money scheming players, but we're not finished yet. Officer Frye is transporting Mousy and Meathead to the Bay St. Louis jail and you, Maggie May, Dr. Banks and his son, plus Amos, are riding with Mac and me. We have a little surprise of our own."

Now as she glanced down at Maggie May lying beside Aunt Jewels' feet, she could have swore the dog was smiling.

Dr. Banks cleared his throat. "Excuse me, but before we leave, Mrs. McKenna, could I relieve you of my dog?"

Bea looked puzzled.

"It's alright Bea, dear," Aunt Jewels laughed, while she reached into the bodice of her dress. "This is the little gadget they all were after also!"

"What is it?" Bea said, "or do I dare ask?"

"I'll be glad to explain," began Dr. Banks. "It's called a 'digital operations gadget', dog, for short. I invented it and I have to install it manually before the shuttle can be launched."

"Wow!" Mac muttered. "You don't say!"

Aunt Jewels began patting her bosom. "And I kept it safe, Bea, right here...over my heart!"

Bea stifled a giggle, as Dr. Banks uttered a few humble words of extreme gratitude.

"Well, now," replied Bea. "Okay, let's get on the road. We have some ground to cover!"

CHAPTER 74

Gerald/Curtis and Jeannie Rose Meet Detective Barry Luce

As they approached the intersection, Jeannie ordered Gerald/Curtis to slow down. Soon the vehicle was crawling at a snail's pace. Up ahead, off to the left, a flash of car lights burst through the darkness.

"That must be him," smiled Jeannie.

"You sure you want to do this?" Asked Gerald/Curtis.

Jeannie sighed, "Oh spare me!"

"Okay, it's your funeral."

Officer Taylor's Patrol Car is Parked a Short Distance Away

Officer Taylor whispered into his car radio, "Sheriff Travis?"

"Yeah, Taylor, what's up?"

"We're down here at Coleman and North Beach. Looks like Sheppard and the girl are meeting with Luce."

"Taylor, call Officer Trace, Bay St. Louis, for back up. She's Officer Frye's partner. Tell her to approach slowly and…no lights!"

"Gotcha!"

On the Beach
With Gerald/Curtis, Jeannie Rose
And Detective Barry Luce

"Who's your friend?" questioned Luce.

"Oh, I knew her awhile back," replied Gerald/Curtis.

"What's your name?"

"Jeannie...Jeannie Rose. That's close enough Mr. Luce. Pull your gun out and toss it over here, at my feet."

"What's going on Sheppard?"

"She's calling the shots!"

"So what's your plan...., what was your name again?" Luce asked.

"Jeannie, Jeannie Rose and first off, Gerald, whose real name is Curtis, is going to tie you up and we'll leave your share of the money."

"Well now honey, that's mighty decent of you."

"I aim to please," she smiled.

"But I don't!" Luce shouted and kicked up sand in her face!

Gerald/Curtis grabbed Jeannie's gun and fired, as Luce lunged for his!

Officer Taylor ran up behind yelling, "Freeze!"

Officer Trace was closing in!

Luce fired, jumped into his car and sped away. Gerald/Curtis threw up his hands, screaming, "Don't shoot!"

"You okay Taylor?" asked Trace.

"Yeah, but the young lady took a bullet in the shoulder. Better contact the Sheriff, Deputy Paulie and Frye that Detective Luce escaped! I'm taking her to the hospital and Mr. Sheppard to jail."

CHAPTER 75

The Shady Rest Funeral Home

Aunt Jewels leaned forward from the back seat and tapped Bea on her shoulder. "Bea?"

"Yes?"

"Why are we sitting in the shadows, watching a funeral home? It's creepy."

"Aunt Jewels, you promised to be quiet."

"And I will. Just answer my question."

"Hush now."

Mac nudged Bea's shoulder. "Look, here comes Sheriff Travis."

"Now maybe I'll get some answers," Aunt Jewels smarted back, while looking at her three male companions and Maggie May.

Bea's eyes flashed! "Aunt Jewels, if you don't behave, I'll take you home right now!"

As the Sheriffs Jeep slowly crept up next to Mac's car, Bea could tell it was Tom Malone in the passenger seat.

"Hi there, you two," said the Sheriff, "are any of the women here yet?"

"Haven't seen hide nor hair of anybody, Jim," Mac replied, shrugging his shoulders.

"Psst...Bea...," remarked Aunt Jewels, poking her niece.

"What is it?"

"That looks like Maudelle's old car coming up the road."

"Bea," continued the Sheriff, "I saw a dim light coming from Fletcher's office, as I drove around the back of the funeral home."

"Maybe Rose is inside already," Bea said.

Sheriff Travis turned towards Tom. "Is the wire in place?"

Tom nodded.

"Okay then, you know what to do."

After exiting the Jeep, Tom gave the Sheriff a thumbs up and ran hurriedly toward the rear entrance. He quietly tiptoed through the narrow passageway, past several viewing parlors to the mirrored ceiling room. While opening the pocket door, his nostrils smelled the faint aroma of jasmine. Rose?"

The flash of light startled him. There stood Rose, with Detective Barry Luce holding a gun to her head. "That's right Tom, come on in and have a seat."

Rose wailed, "Tom, I didn't know…"

"Shut up Rose," demanded Luce. "Tom doesn't want to hear your excuses. It wasn't supposed to be this way, you know. Rose was going to change her plans, weren't you Rose? That's why we killed Horace. Right Rose?"

"Yes," she sobbed.

"And why didn't he die?" sneered Luce, "because Rose did a double-cross. She loaded the gun with blanks!" Luce tighten his grip on Rose. "She also knew that Maudelle was seeing Cyrus; however, she hadn't planned for Charlie to come stumbling in. You see Tom, Horace and Rose discovered their funeral home was sitting on a gold mine, so to speak. They discovered a pocket of natural gas which lay under their property and would bring a kings ransom. So they cooked up their little scheme. Horace would hide out for seven years. However, Rose got antsy and contacted me. Now you Tom, needed this property for the land deal and then you also discovered the documentation about the mineral rights. So you told Rose you were going to take her away to a life of luxury, but Tom, you really weren't going to do that, were you?"

"I don't know what you're talking about."

"Maybe I can shed some light," smiled Luce.

On that note, Maudelle came rushing out of the adjoining bathroom, where she had been hiding. She had used her keys to enter through the Autopsy room.

"Why hello there Maudelle," snickered Luce. "Why don't you stand over there…by your lover."

"Maudelle didn't know whether to be angry or hurt. "Tom, what's he talkin' about? You were supposed to meet me here."

Detective Luce's keen ears picked up a sound. "Everybody in the bathroom…now!" Quickly they filed into the cramped area.

"I told you it would be safe in here," giggled Pearl, as she led Charlie through the pocket door.

While Charlie looked around, he held onto Pearl's hand. "How did you know about this place?"

Pearl kissed his cheek. "I just know, that's all."

Charlie pressed her body close, murmuring, "You are something else Pearl."

"I've told you that all along, honey."

Suddenly the bathroom door opened wide and Detective Luce ordered everybody out.

"Maudelle!" exclaimed Pearl.

Charlie just stood there, dumb founded. "I can explain," he began.

Maudelle simply put up her hand as a signal to stop. "Please…just shut up."

"You might want to know this," Pearl stuttered, Mr.……"

"The name is Luce, Mr. Barry Luce, and please, the both of you move over by your sister and Tom Malone."

"Well Mr. Luce," Pearl continued, "someone is in Mr. Fletcher's office."

CHAPTER 76

Sheriff Jim Travis, Mac and Bea
Enter The Shady Rest
Funeral Home

"Now Aunt Jewels," Bea commanded, "I want you and the three gentlemen to remain in Mac's car. You understand?"

"I don't know why I can't help. I always do, you know."

"I know Aunt Jewels, and I appreciate your help, but Mac and the Sheriff are here."

As Bea silently closed her door, Mac replied, "Do you think that will work?"

Bea grinned, "One never knows about my Aunt Jewels."

"Okay," whispered the Sheriff, "let's go."

Soon the three of them were zigzagging across the back parking lot toward the rear entrance. Tom had left the door unlocked. Once inside, they separated, each covering a specific section. Mac headed toward the Autopsy room, while Bea quietly slipped toward the parlor area. Sheriff Travis was going to check out the light he saw coming from Fletcher's old office.

Walking into the Autopsy room gave Mac the weird feeling that someone was watching him. Slowly he made his way past the stainless steel examination tables and was going to exit, when he was knocked unconscious from behind. Now, the two men began dragging him thru the double doorway and into the bathroom adjacent to the parlor with the mirrored ceiling. They quickly retraced their steps and one returned to the office, just as Sheriff Travis approached.

"Why hello there, Mr. Fletcher," smiled Sheriff Travis. "You are looking very, very well……and alive!"

"Now Jim, I don't want to hurt you. Besides, I've been dead for seven years."

"I heard about that, from the previous Sheriff."

"So, you're going to leave it at that?"

"No, Mr. Fletcher, I'm afraid I can't do that." The Sheriff had no later said those words when he thought he saw five shadows run across the back parking lot, toward the rear entrance.

"Are you going to shoot me, Sheriff?" Horace Fletcher questioned.

"No sir, I'm going to take you into custody."

"For what," Horace laughed, "Impersonating a dead man?"

"No sir, for obstructing justice."

"I certainly don't see anybody else around. So pray tell how are you going to accomplish this feat?"

"I have my ways."

Horace announced confidently, "Rose will arrive any minute now."

"Mr. Fletcher, I believe Rose is already here."

Suddenly there was a commotion coming from the parlor area. "Bea!" yelled the Sheriff.

"I'm okay Jim, I have Barry Luce, Rose, Tom, Maudelle, Charlie and Pearl. Oh yeah, Mac has a lump on his head, but he'll survive."

Sheriff Travis started punching numbers on his cell phone. "Deputy Paulie, I want you and Officer Barney Frye to bring your patrol cars over to The Shady Rest Funeral Home. We are going to be having a lot of company at our jail."

"You have nothing concrete on me, no evidence at all," boasted Barry Luce, "and you know it!"

Tom grinned, while he slowly unbuttoned his shirt. "Mr. Luce, I believe this little device will be convincing in court."

"Why you conniving little snitch!"

Just then a blood-curdling scream came from the hallway to the rear entrance to Horace Fletcher's office. The first to enter was Aunt Jewels, following by Dr. Horatio Banks and his son. Amos Seals was escorting Cyrus Dedeaux, who had Maggie May's jaw clamped around his leg! "Get this hound off of me!" yelled Cyrus.

"Well now folks, that just about completes the picture!" smiled Sheriff Travis.

Within ten minutes, Deputy Paulie and Officer Barney Frye arrived and transported the entire group down to the Bay St. Louis jail.

Conclusion
Christmas Day

"I want to thank you Ms. Barbara for your wonderful hospitality!" Aunt Jewels gushed. "This meal was fantastic! Wasn't it Bea?"

"Really," smiled Barbara, "it's the least the three of us could do for everyone involved in the return and rescue of Maggie May."

"Actually," said Bea, "it was Bay St. Louis' Officer Barney Frye who is the true hero!"

"Now," continued Barbara, clapping her hands together, "you must tell us how it all came about."

"Well," Sheriff Travis began, "the land beyond the buffer zone of Stennis Space Center, was loaded with a pocket of natural gas that extended all the way to the junction of Rooster and Flat Top Road, including Pearl's Beauty Shop and The Shady Rest Funeral Home. When you mix money and greed, you will have people who will sell their soul for the wealth. Tom Malone was one of those people. Even Detective Barry Luce was involved."

"Jim, explain about the natural gas," asked Bea. "I thought it was just a large massive land deal."

"You didn't see the article in the paper this morning?"

"What article?" Bea quizzed. "As usual, Aunt Jewels retrieved the paper before me."

Sheriff Travis excused himself from the table and took The Lafouchfeye Ledger out of his jacket pocket. "It's right here, on the business page. Would you like to see it?"

"Of course."

"Why don't you read it out loud, you know, to all of us."

The look that Bea gave him would have stopped a train dead on the tracks. "Thanks, I will. Well folks, it's reported here that work on a new road called Flat Top, will begin this summer and be a benefit to Stennis Space Center. The cost of this project..."

"Bea?"

"Now what, Jim?"

"Skip down to where it mentions all the right-of-ways."

"As I was saying, let's see, yes here it is. *This purchase involved mitigation of some 60 acres of wetland and the purchase of right-of-way and mineral rights from over 30 landowners ranging from small property owners to long established businesses including the historic general store once owned by Pappy Rooster and The Shady Rest Funeral Home. It even involved some state and federal lands.* Let me skip down....*it also was discovered that a large pocket of natural gas extending from Sycamore all the way down to Flat Top could easily be tapped. The bonus find would be used for future development. This certainly will add to economic expansion for the eastern edge of Stennis Center and the county.*"

"My, my," Aunt Jewels uttered. "So that's what it was all about." "Mercy," sighed Barbara. "I'm not quite sure how our little Maggie May got involved though."

"Well, ma'am," continued Sheriff Travis, "when Ms. Winslow's Aunt Jewels and her boyfriend Captain Eric VonBoatner, stopped by your gift shop, she believed she lost one of Bea's earrings she had borrowed. She figured it somehow came off when she was petting Maggie May."

"But why would they kidnap her and our dog?" John asked.

"Because," winked Aunt Jewels, "I recognized Dr. Horatio Banks, who they were kidnapping and holding possibly for a large ransom!"

"If I may interrupt you Aunt Jewels," replied Bea, "when Sheriff Travis and I were talking to Detective Luce, I asked him an important question."

"And what was that?" Asked Aunt Jewels.

"Well dear, I wanted to know who was going to give the speech. The real Dr. Banks or the fake one. Mr. Luce quickly told me the fake one. Now, if that was true, you would not have been kidnapped!"

"Isn't my niece clever?" beamed Aunt Jewels. "And another thing," she continued, "you see he invented a little gizmo that only he can insert into that shuttle machine to make it go! Well now, they thought he had dropped it in Maggie May's bedding, but I found it and put it a safe place."

"Where was that, Ms. McKenna?" Dave asked.

Bea covered her brow with her right hand. "Here it comes….," She whispered to herself.

Aunt Jewels face broke into a large grin. "I tucked in my bos…I mean, the bodice of my dress! Clever, huh?"

"Yes ma'am…. I agree with you," smiled Dave. "So what happened then?"

"Well, matey," Mac proudly continued, "Lots of things were happening. People that were supposed to be dead, were not and bones were being discovered with the demolishment of Pearl's Beauty Shop. Those bones were the remains of Joseph Fletcher, the son of Rose and Horace Fletcher and the father of Pearl's children, Timmy and MaeBeth. Pearl never told anybody they were secretly married. Maudelle didn't know that when she killed Joe that night. She let Pearl believe that their father did it. Bea, you did that research, so why don't you explain it, you know, from a women's view."

"Thanks Mac," Bea smiled. "When Charlie started seeing Pearl again, she confessed that she and Joe were married. Joe owned the mineral rights and therefore she was entitled to the wealth that lay underneath the grounds of the funeral home."

"That was the natural gas," interrupted Aunt Jewels.

"That's correct, Aunt Jewels. Now please let me continued. Charlie immediately saw dollar bills dancing before his eyes. After all, he had first liked Pearl, but back then, she didn't pay him any attention, so he settled for Maudelle. When he found out Maudelle was cheating on him with Cyrus Dedeaux, he went crazy and followed her that evening, seven years ago, to The Shady Rest Funeral Home. He didn't see Maudelle and Cyrus, but he did see Detective Barry Luce and Rose drag Rose's husband Horace Fletcher out of the back of the 1927 Model T. Ford, taking him through the rear entrance and propping him up in his office chair. Afterwards, both he and Bubba watched as Detective Luce pushed the Model T. Ford over to the rear of the lot. It was Jeannie Rose who told me later, that Bubba had knocked Charlie down and then helped Maudelle carry him to her car. Of course, what Detective Luce didn't know, was that he hadn't killed Mr. Fletcher. Rose had given him a starter gun loaded with blanks! After the inquest, Rose persuaded Cyrus to take the blame. Cyrus was sentenced for Horace's murder. Rose had a closed casket and told everybody she had her husband's body cremated. Nobody was the wiser.

Now Horatio Banks Jr., discovered some new DNA evidence that would clear Cyrus Dedeaux and he was released. Rose was frantic, so she contacted Detective Luce, who thought he and Rose were still going away together, once he got his share of the money."

"That Rose was something else, wasn't she, Barbara?" Aunt Jewels blurted out.

Bea sweetly murmured, "Aunt Jewels."

"Sorry, please continue."

"Thank you dear. As I was saying, Detective Luce had Bubba pitch a vagrant over the side of his boat, with Horatio Banks Jr's identification, so they would believe he was dead. It worked for a little while, but Dr. Nathan Tate was dogmatic and he cleared that up......fast! Thanks to Mac however, when he talked to the Bridge Master, Lucille Tinsley, she recalled whom, what and when. Yes, I'm afraid larceny and greed was in everybody's heart, except Jeannie Rose. She just wanted revenge for her brother Bennie's death by Curtis Burras Alias Gerald Sheppard. Actually, all of them are talking to their lawyers and trying to turn state's evidence against each other. Aunt Jewels, what's that they say about honor and thieves?"

Aunt Jewels giggled, "They say, there is none! Now I must add that Maggie May helped."

"What do you mean, by 'helped'?" John asked.

"Why John," Aunt Jewels began. "When the four of us, plus Maggie May entered the rear entrance and realized Cyrus Dedeaux was going to shoot Horace Fletcher, I screamed and Maggie May grabbed Cyrus' leg and held on! Immediately he dropped the gun!"

"I'm curious," John replied, "Why did Cyrus Dedeaux want to kill Horace Fletcher? After all, didn't y'all just say that lawyer fellow, Horatio Banks Jr. got him off the first time he was convicted?"

"You are absolutely right John," smiled Aunt Jewels. "Again, Rose was involved. She was seeing Cyrus Dedeaux also, and told him that he couldn't be convicted of killing a dead man."

"I agree with Barbara," John replied, "that Rose was quite a woman." Now he looked down at mild Maggie May, lying comfortably on her plaid bedding. "Well girl, you do have an aggressive side after all."

Just then, Sheriff Travis grabbed his stemmed wine glass and stood up. "I would like to propose a toast. A Merry Christmas and Happy New Year to friends and family around this table. May we enjoy each others company and friendship forever!"

"Hear....hear!" Aunt Jewels laughed.

Suddenly Maggie May began howling.

"I think," Bea winked at Sheriff Travis, "that Maggie May thinks you forgot her!"

"Not on your life Maggie May," smiled the sheriff, after all, it sure is a dog gone Christmas!"

978-0-595-41098-9
0-595-41098-7